D0761397

Too Much on the Inside

Too Much on the Inside

Danila Botha

QUATTRO BOOKS

Copyright © 2015, Danila Botha and Quattro Books Inc.

The use of any part of this publication, reproduced, transmitted in any form or by any means, electronic, mechanical, photocopying, or otherwise stored in an electronic retrieval system without the prior consent (as applicable) of the individual author or the designer, is an infringement of the copyright law.

The publication of *Too Much on the Inside* has been generously supported by the Canada Council for the Arts and the Ontario Arts Council.

 Canada Council for the Arts   Conseil des Arts du Canada

 ONTARIO ARTS COUNCIL
CONSEIL DES ARTS DE L'ONTARIO
an Ontario government agency
un organisme du gouvernement de l'Ontario

Author photo: Karen Schmidt
Editor: Sandra Kasturi
Cover design and typography: Natasha Shaikh

Library and Archives Canada Cataloguing in Publication

Botha, Danila, author
    Too much on the inside / Danila Botha.

ISBN 978-1-927443-75-0 (pbk.)

    I. Title.

PS8647.A94L66 2015   C813'.6   C2015-902327-0

Published by Quattro Books Inc.
Toronto
www.quattrobooks.ca

Printed in Canada

"I have all this stuff welling up in me, and this stuff to say and I can't get it out, it all seems so important.

And then when it bunches up like that, up against my front teeth, itching to get out, I just get stuck. They don't know I have too much to say, that's why."
—Cathleen With, *Skids* (from "Marvellous Madame Mim")

"Women will put up with any amount of torture
To make a relationship 'work'
I only did the torturing
Because I could"
—Aryan Kaganof, "Raison d'être"

"I panic when I can't see the stars. I panic when the sun is a central smog and my direction is a stoned pigeon wrapped in a map."
—Toast Coetzer, "The Highveld"

"Everything in this world has a heart. The heart itself has its own heart."
—Rabbi Nachman of Breslov

Nicki

People open up to me a lot.

I work at a bar, the 9:00 p.m. to 2:00 a.m. shift most of the time, and around 11:00 p.m. people start to talk.

There's a guy who cross-dresses, wears the clothes his ex left behind, panties and tights under his jeans to work when he misses her, and full-out drag—her dresses and eye shadow and bras—when he's sitting in what used to be their home and he's tempted to call her.

I've heard about a woman who has sex with another woman a lot despite being married to a man.

I've heard about men who don't love their wives or girlfriends, women who don't love one or all of their kids.

None of it is shocking anymore. What I've learned is, what people want is to tell someone, anyone, their problems. Even quiet people don't seem to mind telling a stranger. They want to talk without being judged, to process things by hearing them said out loud. All they want to know is that someone is listening.

Sometimes I offer customers a drink on me, a tissue, sometimes I offer them some drugs. *Our bartender can hook you up*, I tell them, and he usually does.

Sometimes people ask about me, but I never tell them anything.

Where would I begin?

You have to have real clarity in your life to be able to talk about it.

It's easier not to say anything, or to make it up.

It's easier to smile, to ask people what they need, and to give it to them.

Having a job where you serve people is much easier than being yourself.

It doesn't involve any real thinking or acknowledging of your own needs.

When I leave the bar, I take the long walk home, past the white, sky-high buildings that glow in the dark from the inside against the star-free sky.

The only stars that people are interested in around here are the ones on their TVs. TV hosts and members of bands I've never heard of. No one misses nature here. No one misses the quiet.

When I get home, at around 4:00 a.m., my boyfriend is usually still at work.

He doesn't get home until 5:30 or 6:00 a.m.

I wait up for him most nights, and then neither of us talks much about what we did.

In Israel, one of the most commonly used expressions is *ein li coakh*—I don't have the strength.

We collapse into bed together, ready to start again the next night.

We don't talk about the details because it's pointless.

We don't talk about ourselves because we both have too much to say.

Dez

Toronto feels like nowhere I've ever lived—a blood-pumping organ that keeps everyone in it alive, a girl whose limbs are easy to follow, but whose hidden arteries snake and make everyone feel like they're in on a secret. There's a relentless pace, a desire in people's eyes I've never seen before, to land here and conquer.

That's what excited me most, at first—the number of other immigrants, the possibility of success, and the sheer amount of choices, restaurants and music that I hadn't known existed—if I wanted spicy shrimp pho or a warm churro dusted with cinnamon and sugar, if I wanted to hear live blues, or local hip hop, if I wanted to get drunk then eat the greasiest udon noodles and dim sum at two in the morning to stave off a hangover—it was easy.

This city is so cleanly designed, but in my first week, I got lost. I was supposed to meet a friend from Brazil at Yonge Street and St. Clair Avenue, but I got off the subway at St. Clair Avenue West. I didn't know the difference. I stared at the map, the long, curving yellow track of the subway line, but I didn't know which way I was supposed to be going. I didn't feel confident asking for directions. Even though I studied English in school, and in university, I made hundreds of mistakes when I first got here. I didn't know how Canadians really talked. I didn't know any slang and I got so many expressions wrong. I told someone on the street that I had a doubt, instead of a question. I told someone else I lost my bus instead of saying I missed it. I could tell they were trying not to laugh when they corrected me. I could also tell that a lot of Canadian girls thought my mistakes were cute. I was happy that people were so polite here.

I walked out of the station, through the park. I passed the Loblaws and Shoppers Drug Mart. A girl in a short skirt was leaning up against the wall of a Jamaican restaurant, smoking.

Hi, I said to her, all shaky and hesitant. I smiled. *Can I— Can I have—a—a cigarette?*

She laughed. *Quando você se moveu aqui,* she said quickly: when did you move here? She had a nice gap between her two front teeth, like that model from France. She had shapely thighs. I felt relief like never before, like my limbs were caving in, and there was an expensive leather couch behind me waiting to catch me.

Semana passada, I said, a week ago. It felt so good to speak my language to a stranger.

Wow, she said. She had a great accent, Portuguese mixed with Canadian, mixed with something else, something I'd never heard. *Sou de Portugal, dos Açores,* she said. That was it, she was from the Azores. I'd only ever been to Lisbon.

Eu sou Brasileiro, I told her, I'm Brazilian.

Eu sei, she answered, I know. I can tell.

She invited me into the Jamaican restaurant she worked in. *It is out of this world,* she told me in English, and I knew it'd be good from the way she looked at me. She served me spicy oxtail soup, curried goat, and stewed peas.

Minha boca esta queimando, I said, my mouth is on fire.

She put a glass of water in front of me. *Somente espere,* she said, just wait.

She wouldn't let me tip her when I got up to pay. *Não quero uma ponta,* she said, I don't want a tip, not that kind. She smiled, and wrote her number and address down for me on a napkin. She lived just down the street, on Vaughan Road. *Venha para duas horas,* she said, come in two hours. And I did.

It was my first time having sex in Canada, and it was amazing. She had such a hot body, and she wanted to do it with the lights on. She didn't want to know anything about me—she seemed like she liked casually hooking up, like she did it all the time, which just made her seem hotter. She'd call and leave me dirty messages on my cell phone, and the thrill of getting caught seemed hotter than anything. Her name was Luisa. I kept seeing her on and off for two years after that, until she found herself a real boyfriend. I wasn't worried. I knew I'd have lots of encounters with other women.

The city is always pulsing, and I feel it, there's always adrenaline coursing through my veins. I was overcome all the time with the desire to explore, to understand. I wanted to get it: I wanted to know where all these people came from, what they were saying, where they were going. Reality seemed different from what I knew and I wanted to experience it. I was starving for a taste of everything—every kind of music, and food and drink, every kind of woman of every kind of culture, especially the ones I'd never heard of.

I didn't work for my first two years here. I went to ESL classes in the mornings, first at the government-funded one near where I was living, and then at an expensive private language school in Yorkville. I made friends with students from Korea, Japan and Mexico, and we spent our lunch times battling to communicate in English. I taught them some Brazilian expressions, like *viajar na maionese*, to travel in the mayonnaise, which we say when someone says something really crazy, and *descascar o abacaxi*, to peel the pineapple, which we say when we have to solve a problem. They laughed and laughed. All my real jokes got lost in translation.

After class I'd wander around on my own, observing, trying to pick up phrases and mannerisms. I'd talk to strangers as much as possible.

I watched older women in the middle of the day in Chinatown, grabbing at vegetables and dried shrimp in cardboard boxes on the sidewalk, bargaining maybe, it was hard to know. I never heard one word of English, and I wasn't sure if I would've understood them if I had. It was the accent and the speed. But I understood their urgency.

I once talked to a Brazilian banker, Fernando, on the subway. He worked in finance, on Front Street, he said, and he was happy to show me his office.

I was just like you, a few years ago, he said. He worked at the headquarters of a major bank. The building had impressive marble floors, and two sets of elevators that led into their South and North towers. I was surprised by how many South American names were on the desks; how many Dos Santoses and Ferreiras there were. I knew I wanted a different kind of success—a less corporate, more alternative version. Still, it was reassuring to know it was possible.

I started talking to three university students one afternoon, at a taco place near Bloor and Spadina. The guy wore one of those Guatemalan Mayan wool sweaters in Rasta colours. The girls had that hippie student look—messy ponytails, socks with Birkenstocks. They were talking about Nietzsche, whom I'd actually read.

They asked me if I was new to Toronto, and I nodded. They offered to take me with them to a drum circle in Trinity Bellwoods Park. We took two streetcars there and walked down a hill to an area they called the dog bowl, and found a huge crowd of kids, laughing and playing different kinds of drums. Some kids were dancing in the middle of the circle they'd formed. A girl was twirling a hula hoop, first around her waist, and then each of her toned legs, and a guy was waving a rope with fire on the end of it. Above, in the area between the buildings and a street, a girl was sitting on a giant swing, swinging topless, while a crowd gathered around her.

What is she doing, I asked a guy who was gawking next to me.

He shrugged. *It's performance art.*

I grinned. *I like it. Does this happen here a lot*, I asked him.

Yeah, he said. *I mean, there's also farmers' markets and arts festivals. There's a Portugal Day festival here every year that's pretty awesome. There's a Portuguese community along Dundas, over on the other side of the park.*

I smiled. I wanted to fit in, but I was still happy when people recognized my accent. I walked past a girl on her knees giving a guy a blow job in the bushes on my way out. I talked to two girls who gave me their numbers, and least three people tried to sell me weed. I was too exhilarated to get high. It was my first time in the area and I was in love with it.

I kept walking east on Queen Street for blocks, then a little more west. Everyone had such wild style. I passed a guy with a handlebar moustache, wearing a red velvet blazer and gold glasses, and a girl in black leather pants and a corset, with a tattoo that said, *if you don't live for something, you'll die for nothing* popping out across the tops of her breasts. I heard punk and goth music blasting out of club doors, saw bars that were upscale but quirky. My city, Belo Horizonte, is known as the Brazilian capital of the *boteco*, or bar scene. We have more bars per capita than anywhere in Brazil. We even use the term *boteco-copo-sujo*, or dirty cup pub.

I see the dirt mixed with the glitter, the open, chaotic energy of Toronto and I know it's the place for me. I want to live in this city, and I know that as soon as I can, I want to open my own bar here.

Marlize

The sun is shining—I can see glimpses of it when I look up at his blinds.

It casts thin white stripes across his sheet-creased face. He's clutching a corner of the blanket close to his cheek. He looks like he's five years old, the blanket balled up in his fist.

Looking at his hands brings it all back.

I think of those thick fingers deep inside me, two at a time.

I'm having a hard time breathing.

I keep rubbing my eyes. I wish I could look at him, this room, this hook-up, and think, *This is my life, I wanted this.*

There are tequila bottles, some half empty, some broken on the counters and floor. The kitchen linoleum is covered with salt. It feels like coarse Karoo sand under my feet. I found one of my socks, purple with a bloodstain on one toe from a blister I had from wearing heels, but I can't find the other one. I find my tank top and my panties under my shoes, but I don't know where my bra is.

There are mascara smudges under my eyes; I see them when I look in the bathroom mirror.

There is a cut on my arm, just under my elbow.

I trace it with my finger.

He's still asleep. Since it's a studio apartment, and the door is open, I can see him from the bathroom.

He has the sheet wrapped around him, tangled through his legs. He's naked underneath it.

It starts coming back, like vomit rising in the back of my throat.

I met him at the bar. He's Australian. He's a painter called Joe. He asked me to come to his house party when I finished work, and I'd been feeling restless and crawling out of my skin with boredom, so I came.

I knew what I was getting myself into. He didn't seem dodgy. He reminded me of surfer dudes in South Africa, the kind of guys who say *Howzit Bru, awesome waves in Muizenberg*, and not much else. He's what Canadians would call a bro. There was something comforting about how familiar it all felt, and the fact that we had nothing in common made it even better.

My first time didn't really count. I'm almost twenty-two. I need to get over it already.

I think I might like my boss, Dez. Everything about him, from his tanned skin to his fawn eyes, is so warm. Sometimes I think I want to sleep with him, too. The more experience I have the better. I want to have sex again and this time I want to like it.

Joe's friends and I quietly judged each other. We didn't talk much. They looked at me and probably thought *reserved*, maybe *stuck up*. I looked at them and thought, *idiots*. He pulled me close to him around 1:30 a.m. He said we should dance. They were playing that song "Frontier Psychiatrist" by The Avalanches. He kissed me. I pulled away, leaned against the open window and half considered jumping out.

Joe told me he always thought I was hot, way hotter than the other girls there. He had to drink a lot to be able to make a move, he said. He thought about it whenever he came into the bar, but didn't think I'd actually go out with him. I tried not to laugh. It was ridiculous. He was hot, blond and tanned, with a tribal armband tattoo. He had no trouble getting women. I wanted his words to be true. *You're too suspicious of men*, I told myself. *He could be fun.*

I begged him not to talk about sports. Australians always wanted to compare South Africa's cricket and rugby scores with their own. I couldn't think of anything more boring.

He leaned forward, brushed a piece of hair out of my face. *You don't know how hard it is*, he said, *to find someone that you find interesting. You're an interesting girl, you know. I really like your accent.*

I looked at him, stood there swaying from snorting too much coke, trying to act like I did this all the time, this was all so *kiff*, and so was I, so cool.

He took me to his bedroom, kissing me, gently pushing me into the wall behind me. He was a little rough when he took off my clothes.

I like him, I told myself, over and over. *I know him. I know him enough, anyway. I wanted this.*

It started to feel good. I found myself moaning, not wanting it to be over. I felt free for the first time in a long time. I closed my eyes, heart pounding in my ears, blood pumping below my waist, tears falling that I didn't notice until after. He didn't notice at all, or didn't act like he did.

That was intense, was all he said when he was finished.

His apartment was on the twelfth floor, the top floor of the building. He had a balcony on the roof that had space for everyone at the party. After we had a few drinks looking out over the city, he took me downstairs, to the apartment, and closed the door. I didn't know how to act so I improvised. He asked me to stay the night. I didn't have enough money to take a cab so I did.

This morning, I'll walk then take the streetcar home.
I find my pants on the floor near the foot of the bed, find my jacket on the pile near the door, put my shoes on even though I only have one sock.

He doesn't wake up as I close the door and a part of me feels relieved. In the living area of his studio, there is a massive canvas that all his guests were encouraged to draw on all night. I grab a black marker and write the word *vryheid* in the corner in capital letters. Freedom. Then underneath it, in smaller letters, I write *dankie vir alles*. Thanks for everything. I don't need to sign it.

I find myself smiling as the sun hits my face when I step outside, onto the street.

Lukas

We meet in a record store on Queen Street. It has a neon green wall outside and the store logo's orange and red. I think I'm gonna go blind just lookin' at it. Inside, there's tons of records I never heard of, especially the staff picks. I ask this girl who works there, who has puffy hair and thick black-framed glasses, what this hip hop album I pick up sounds like, and she rambles on about early nineties conscious hip hop in Philadelphia. I have no idea what she's sayin'. It reminds me of Taz Records, this vinyl store in Halifax, crossed with that movie *High Fidelity*. A girl in front of me is lookin' for a CD, some young British band with gorillas or monkeys or some kinda animal in the title. The metrosexual hipster who's sittin' at the cash register is bein' a douche. Maybe his skin-tight jeans are crushing his balls. The girl tries to pay for it and he sneers at her choice.

Her smile fades.

I'm standin' behind her in line, and I whisper, *Don't ever trust any guy who wears eyeliner. Plus, he's got a messenger bag, for fuck's sake. It's like the Douchebag Uniform. Trust me, it's not you.*

I put down the Pantera and Machine Head albums I'd been planning to buy. *I won't buy here on principle anymore*, I tell her. *They can't sell me that bill of goods.*

She laughs at that, looks up at me, she's maybe 5'3" or 5'4", almost a foot shorter than me, and asks, *Where are you from?*

I smile back. *How can you tell?*

You're friendlier than the people here, she says. *And you actually say what you're thinking.*

I smile. *You're from away too, aren't ya*, I ask her.

She nods slowly, like she isn't completely sure what I'm askin'. I like her already.

There's something electric about someone believing you're the real deal.

I decide to ask her right then if she'll go with me for coffee down the street. She says yes. She says she doesn't have to be at work for another three hours.

I like the way she orders her coffee black—no sugar or cream, nothin' extra.

She's different to other girls I meet in this city who order soy lattes, matcha green tea chai frappuccinos and some other stupid, expensive drinks they expect you to pay for.

Her coffee comes to, like, a dollar fifty, and she won't even order a pastry, or a donut, even though I offer to get her one twice.

I check her out as we stand in line. Her dress is too loose— it's one of those hippie numbers that don't let you see what a girl's body actually looks like.

I like her green eyes, the way she isn't wearin' any makeup so you can actually see her face. I like that she's kinda messy-lookin'—long, tangled hair, what we call all mops and brooms back home. She definitely has an exotic look.

So where are ya from, I ask her, expecting her to say somewheres in Europe. *France?* She seems French.

Israel, she says, and I'm surprised. I never met anyone from there before.

What language do you speak, I ask.

She says, *Hebrew*, and I make a mental note to look it up online when I get home.

Are you Jewish, I ask her.

She shrugs. *Well technically, yes, but I'm not religious. My parents are Orthodox.* She looks up at the cross I'm wearin' around my neck. *Are you Christian?*

No, I say quickly then ramble, *well I mean, my mom's Anglican, and she got it for me, but I wear it more for sentimental reasons than anything. I haven't taken it off in years. I haven't been to church in a long time though. I guess I'm not really religious either.*

She doesn't really seem that surprised I thought she was French. *Everyone in Canada does*, she says. *It's the way we roll our 'r's' that sounds similar to people here. Where are you from?* she asks me.

Have you heard of Halifax? I ask her. She shakes her head. *It's on the east coast. Like a two-hour flight from here. But I'm from the country, a couple hours from there.*

19

Really? I used to live in the country too, with my ex-boyfriend. We lived near the ocean.

What do you do here, I ask her.

I work four days a week at a bar near to here, you know CDRR?

It's a dive bar down on Queen West, near the Gladstone. I'll tell you right fuckin' now, they call it STD RR. The girls are greasy as fuck. Everyone goes to hook up, and it's totally normal to walk into the bathroom and hear people moanin' and the stall walls thumpin'. I once seen a girl with her skirt pulled the full way up go flyin' through a stall door. The guy's pants were down too. I guess he must have pushed too hard, or maybe the lock was weak. It was pretty funny. Lots of blow in their bathrooms too. I hear the owner sells it, but I never buy from him.

They have pretty good music, I'll give 'em that, classic R&B and rock on the jukebox, good local rock and punk bands. Pretty cheap beer on tap, good kitchen-sink style nachos and poutine that remind of this place in Dartmouth. CDRR is really popular and packed lately, so I go less.

Never seen her there before.

Yeah. It's like ten minutes from my apartment. When do you work? I ask. *I go there all the time.*

During the week, on Tuesdays and Fridays, she says. *And on weekends. I just started last month. Where do you live?*

Parkdale. On Cowan Street.

She smiles. *Oh, I've seen that street. That is close. I like Parkdale.*

Yeah? I like it too. It's got lots of character.

She nods. *It reminds me of this neighbourhood, Florentine, in South Tel Aviv. It's exciting and colourful and you feel like it's on the verge of exploding with creativity.*

Yeah, I say. *I get what you mean. This part of Queen always reminds me of Gottigen Street in Halifax. It's gritty and full of life. So what do you do besides work at CDRR?* I ask.

I take photography classes at the Toronto School of Art, off Spadina. I think I might want to be a photographer.

I have to see your photos sometime, I tell her, and she smiles, twirls a piece of her hair around her finger, like she's shy all of a sudden.

What do you do? she asks me.

I hesitate then decide to tell her. *I'm a janitor at Toronto General Hospital. It's literally pretty shit. Patients shit their beds and you have to clean it up, change their sheets. People are barfin' or bleedin' all over the floor and you have to make it look like it never happened. I work shitty hours too, really early mornings that start at 5:00 a.m., or really late nights. But the pay is pretty good.*

She's watching me intently. *It must feel good,* she says, to *help people by making their stay in the hospital a little nicer.*

I nod, feed her some lines about makin' a difference. She seems all eager to believe it for some reason.

I don't tell her that a youth worker, who looked at my case and pulled some strings because they felt sorry for me, found me the job.

I don't tell her about what I did all those years ago that got me into this situation. I don't tell her about how I fantasize sometimes about having a normal job. I don't tell her I can't apply for one unless I wanna work at Timmy's.

I let her think I'm some noble guy who wants to work hard and help people.

I like her so that's how it starts, right from the get-go. I can't tell her, 'cause she would bolt, and who could blame her?

So I don't say anything, and she comes over before work, and we listen to the Beatles, *Revolver* and *Magical Mystery Tour,* her choices, smoke a bowl of weed, and fool around.

Her body's great. She has a great ass, and she's totally unshaved—all dark curly hairs. I never seen that before, but it turns me on. She's so low-maintenance, so not Toronto.

I still don't tell her anything and she doesn't ask. She seems to be into an idea of what I could be, and I like that. I like when girls believe I got potential.

She moves in with me not too long after. Not long after that, she tells me she loves me for the first time.

You don't know me, I want to yell, but I don't.

I just say, *I love you too.*

It's kinda hard not to love her.

Me, on the other hand, if she knew, she'd be gettin' the fuck away from me, so fast. I want her to keep tellin' me she loves me. I wanna be the kind of guy that's decent and trustworthy.

I wanna pretend until it becomes the truth.

I wanna hold on as hard as I can until she leaves me.

Dez

She comes over while I'm wiping down the counter. It's quiet, the music is on low volume, an eighties hair metal ballad, so she doesn't have to shout, and when she speaks, I can hear her.

"Every Rose Has Its Thorn"? I hate this kind of music, she says, wrinkling up her nose.

I laugh. *Uai,* I say. *I love Poison. Come on, who doesn't love cheesy hair metal?* I grab a beer mug I should be drying, turn it upside down and serenade her.

She starts giggling, flashing the kind of white-toothed North American smile that kills me. Her lips are glossy.

Her eyes drop to my nametag. *Dez can't be your real name,* she says.

Nope. It's a nickname, comes from my last name, Da Silva.

What's your real name then, she says, leans in closer.

What's yours?

I asked you first.

Okay, but you should know, only my mom ever calls me that. I pause dramatically. *It's Leonardo.*

Leonardo, she repeats. *I like it.*

Leonahdo, I say. *We say our 'r's' like 'h's' in Brazil.*

It's a nice name, she says. *Like DiCaprio.*

Or like the Ninja Turtle, I say.

She laughs again, flashes those teeth. *What does she call you for short?*

Leo, I say.

Lay-o, she repeats.

Good pronunciation, I tell her. I can smell her perfume, something with vanilla, Gaultier, I think.

Can I call you that? She flutters her eyelashes at me, eyes all big and hopeful.

We'll see, I say, and grin. *If you're good.*

She leans in so close her lips almost touch my chin. *And if I'm bad?*

I smile, tell her I'll be finished here in twenty minutes. She says she'll wait, writes her number down on the back of a receipt someone left on the counter.

I probably won't use it, but it's a cute thing to do. Her name is Marcy.

You're cute, I tell her, and she smiles one more time, twirls a piece of her hair around her finger.

She's wearing one of those low-cut tops that almost shows her nipples when she bends over.

I've had my eye on her all night but haven't done a thing.

The best way to pick up is to make eye contact and smile, but make them come to you. Toronto is an easy place to pick up women. I'm overcome all the time with the desire to explore, to see, to understand. I want to get it: I want to know where all these people came from, what they're saying, where they're going. Reality seems different here. I want to experience it. I want to take a taste of everything—every kind of music, and food and drink, every kind of woman of every kind of culture, especially the ones I've never heard of.

Marlize

I learned to swim when I was five. We had a pool in our garden like every other family we knew in Durbanville. I knew we weren't rich, like my mom's friend who owned a winery in Franschhoek and drove a Mercedes. We were comfortable but it didn't occur to me to feel privileged. I wore pink floaties that smelled like melting plastic around my chubby arms and coconut sunscreen all over. I splashed and kicked, practised blowing bubbles with my face in the water. I had daydreams about being half salmon, a fluffy blonde girl with brown eyes and a coral mermaid's tail. Instead of tasting like chlorine, the water would be green and taste like cream soda. I wanted to drink it in by the bucketful.

My folks would always be there too, my mom floundering next to me in a striped red and blue full piece *cozzy*, my dad in a Speedo with a full chest of hair. My dad had a big eighties moustache—he was from Bloem, what they called *Snor* city, or moustache city. Even now, Bloemfontein is like 1989 everyday. But when I was five it was 1989, so it was okay.

Everyone got along then without pretending. We'd go to the beach on Saturdays, Bloubergstrand most often, eating picnic lunches, rolls covered in sand, crunchy and salty. When I was five, I could finally swim with the older kids in the sea, instead of sitting under the umbrella, listening to my mom and all the *tannies*, her friends who were like aunts, *skinner*, or gossip about people and things I didn't understand. Every so often they'd look at me and say *Ag shame man, she's so sweet*. They'd stare at me furtively, whisper when I made eye contact, cackle about friends and neighbours, someone having an affair. I could run in the sun by the water out of eyeshot. I could swim, get *klapped* by the waves, get *moered* into rocks, drown if I wanted. No one was really watching me, because no one had to, I was okay. My sister was supposed to watch me, and maybe she did, but I never noticed her. It was the most exciting feeling I'd ever had. It felt like anything was possible. I felt independent.

Swimming at the beach was the first time I remember feeling free.

Nicki

He always talks about how much he misses being near water. Sometimes we go for walks at the Lakeshore, or at Sunnyside Beach. Sometimes I go by myself just to take photos. Today the lake at Sunnyside is the colour of cigarette ash, with a tiny drop of blue, like the blue was an afterthought, an accident on a paint palette.

When we fight he goes out. He goes for a walk, goes to work, or the convenience store, anywhere but here. He can't get away from me fast enough when we argue.

I always think, *when you argue at least you know where you really stand. At least everything is clear.*

I didn't realize it, but what I want is a relationship and an apartment and a life that feels like home. Something permanent. Something I can get angry with, or get dark with, or lazy with, that will still be intact no matter what.

He yells at me. He says he's sick of my optimism, my trying to see the best in a pile of shit. He's frustrated with his job. I keep trying to think of solutions. I keep being my annoying cheery self.

Fuck right off, Lady Fix-It, he snaps.

He tells me I see things in him that don't really exist.

He doesn't talk about anything that he sees in me.

We've been living together for five months, but it's because of my lack of organization, the way I do things and spontaneously hope for the best. I was only planning to stay a few nights, but then I never left and now he never asks me to.

It's strange, when things get really bad, I worry that I'm being a *frayerit,* Israeli slang for the most gullible sucker, for staying with him. I think, *what's wrong with me, I should just leave, why don't I,* but then fear paralyzes me. What if there's nowhere better to go? What if all men are the same? What if every situation I walk into leaves me feeling this alone?

He doesn't understand that this ability to move countries all the time, these attempts to be happy, it takes effort. I have to try hard to be this person.

Sometimes I want to kick and scream and break things—the wall, the TV, my bones.

Sometimes I'm convinced that Lukas doesn't know the first thing about me.

He doesn't want to. He's not the only one.

Marlize, this girl I wait tables with, tells me that my openness is just too much. We are dropping dead tired, it's after 1:00 a.m. We're wiping down tables. I'm trying to make conversation. She says she feels like shit. I tell her it doesn't show and reach over to give her a hug and she pulls me off the way you pull a mosquito off your arm before you squash it to death. She looks like she wants to crush me with the heel of her motorcycle boots.

Ag, you know, it's too much for me, she says, *all this. I don't even know you.*

She stops when she sees my jaw drop.

Shame, you're trying to be nice, she says, seeming almost human for a second. *I just don't know you at all,* she says coldly and walks off without looking back.

Dez, my boss, does a good imitation of her. She's South African, but she rolls her 'r's' like she's Spanish. It's actually hard to understand her sometimes.

My fight with Lukas ends late, around 3:00 a.m. We have one bedroom, and a living room with a foldout couch. He goes to sleep on the couch when we fight. I pretend to be sleeping, not crying, and he watches reality TV or porn on his computer until 7:00 a.m., when I get up to go to school. I'm taking art courses, and one ESL class at a college nearby. My English is good, I know; I work on it like crazy, but sometimes, weird translations come out, mistakes that don't seem like mistakes, but make Canadians laugh.

We are fighting, and he says, *You don't have a fucking clue, do you?*

And I yell back, *I have a clue,* which is what you say in Hebrew when someone says *Ein lach musag,* you don't have a clue, you say *yesh li musag,* I have a clue.

He starts laughing at me, hysterically, and I start screaming out of frustration, crying and screaming, and he says I am hysterical.

Why don't you ever go anywheres, he yells. *I'm sick of bein' the one to leave.*

I don't have where to go, I yell back.

I don't have SOMEWHERES to go, Nicki, he screams. *Somewheres. Anywheres. God, why don't you just learn to speak English?*

He grabs his coat and slams the door behind him. It's 10:30 a.m. and he still hasn't come home yet.

Sometimes it's clear that he doesn't get me at all.

Marlize

When I was seven I'd tap my feet to songs on the radio. My family would drive to resorts with beaches during Christmas break, places like Langebaan or Paternoster. It was hot, and windy, and we'd sit in the backseat, the leather sticking to the backs of our legs, windows open, radio blasting, the wind whipping my eardrums. My sister Claudette would sing along to whatever songs were playing, "The Locomotion," "I Think We're Alone Now." Loud. *Ag, maar sy's oulik.* Oh, she's so cute. My mom would melt no matter how off-key she was.

My dad would roll his eyes, pretending to focus on the road, but I could see him smiling in the car's side mirror, trying not to, but giving in anyway. Claudette had that effect on everyone.

I remember my feet moving instinctively, tapping wildly, like it was the most natural thing. I loved to move, even then. It took me outside of myself, outside of wherever I was, to a place full of swirling colours and easy movements. Hours could pass that felt like seconds.

I couldn't sit still when I started school either.

I'd get up from my chair, sashay through the desks around me, shimmy through the school corridors when I needed the bathroom. Maths was the worst. I couldn't focus or retain information.

My friend Lanelle used to try to explain it to me after school. *Check*, she'd say, *just pay attention, man. Stop with all the blady moving around.*

When I needed to work something out, I'd tap my feet against the floorboards, flex and point my calves and ankles without realizing it.

The principal and teacher met with my mother to give her the news: *Perhaps, Mevrou Van Zyl, Mrs Van Zyl, what Marlize needs is dance lessons.* They made some recommendations, and my mother signed me up.

I was a natural. Ballet became my whole life. It was strange and fantastic to be rewarded for doing something I actually loved. I kept getting better and better, doing recitals, practising five or six hours a day. High school was a blur of tutus, pink and black, blisters and ankles that bled, muscles and stretching, challenges I won, and ones I lost, experimenting with jazz and modern and tap.

My goal was to go professional—to study dance at the University of Cape Town for a year, and then be good enough to join the Cape Town City Ballet—the best dance company in the country. I'd taken classes with them for years, and their director had told me that I was a shoe-in.

I'd watched every performance they gave—*The Firebird, Swan Lake, The Nutcracker*, and imagined myself up there.

Visualize, my teacher Anneli would always tell me. *You have to visualize to actualise.*

Ballet gave me a focus and a purpose. It gave me a feeling of structure and confidence. It was what I was supposed to be able to do for another ten years, and then I imagined I'd open a dance school.

It was supposed to be my life.

When they broke into our house, they stabbed me in the thighs then left me tied to my desk chair with thick rope that cut across my legs. My feet turned blue because the ropes were tied too tightly, and were left on too long. The nerve damage was the worst part. I permanently lost muscle control and the ability to hold poses for long enough to ever get it back.

My dad and grandparents paid a fortune to send me overseas, to send me away from a place where this happens to people all the time. Their expectations were huge—the dollar was 7.35 to the rand.

I'm here on a student visa—studying Contemporary Arts and Global Studies at Ryerson University. I'm in my second year. I find my classes interesting, but I have no idea what I'm going to do with any of it.

Without dance, I have no identity and no direction. I have no confidence in what I'm capable of.

I don't know how to answer my father when he calls me and asks how things are going. Sometimes I lie—I talk about wanting to go into journalism, or working for a non-profit in the arts. Sometimes I consider telling him the truth—that I miss home. That I don't know why I'm still alive, why I have the privilege of living overseas and having my university taken care of for me.

That sometimes more than anything I long for my old life, for the innocence of believing I am in control of everything. I never say these thoughts out loud.

The closest I come is when my dad says he misses me, and I say, *Ja, you as well.*

I know he can't take hearing how hard it is for me. I tell him what I know he needs to hear.

I like working at the bar because it helps me focus less on what I'd like in the moment. Sometimes that's easier.

The times I spend living instead of thinking are the times that I convince myself that I'm the happiest.

Lukas

Nicki's always askin' me what my life was like growin' up in the Annapolis Valley. It's not that I don't wanna tell her, I just don't know what the fuck to say. It's not exactly a happenin' place.

✦

I spent a lot of time on my grandparents' farm when I was young. They mostly grew fruit, but they had some chickens, a couple of sheep, and a black and white goat that they said could be my own pet. I called him Max, and he was a big suck. He loved to be held when he was little, like a puppy, and even when he got big, with sharp horns and a long white beard, he'd love it if I tried to lift him up. When my grandfather gave him away, the neighbours said they thought Max was gonna die of heartache, and I damn near did too. Seriously, I cried for that goat, and I was thirteen.

My parents got divorced when I was nine and by the time I was thirteen my mom had remarried a guy, was in the Armed Forces like my dad. I guess that happens when you grow up in a small town near a military base. We had to move around a lot—to the UK, to Germany, to the US.

✦

Nicki thinks the army is fuckin' cool even if she won't admit it. Her eyes light up when she talks about her time in the Israeli army, the friends she made, the bonding and all that shit. She spent a lot of her time in an office, never really seein' any action. The way she describes her basic training makes it sound like summer camp—a bunch of teenage girls from all over the country about to share in something exciting and unforgettable. Maybe that's how they market it to people so they can get through it, or maybe that's just Nicki, always smilin', always fightin' to see the good in things.

School was the fuckin' shits. A bunch of my teachers were officers, and schools on the bases were run military style. Everything was on a schedule, had to be done exactly the way they told you. I was always bad at not arguing if I thought something was stupid. I was the class clown who couldn't focus but made other kids laugh. I got angrier and angrier, moving from place to place, not knowing where the hell I was, who to be friends with or how long I'd even be there.

I exploded at a teacher one day. I failed some test and she said she didn't think I could pass that year, so I told her to fuck right off. We kept arguing and I threw three books at her, and one of 'em hit her right in the head. I refused to apologize and they expelled me. My stepdad kicked me out, with a one-way ticket back to the Valley to live with my grandfather.

I met a girl from down home who I went out with, and then lived with for a couple years. I met her in Montreal after I got out of juvie. I got a job in construction, and she worked at a Timmy's near the site. Heather was three years younger than me, but she was by no means innocent.

She was sarcastic and sexy. She liked school about as much as me, so neither of us exactly finished. I got my GED after a while but she only got her grade eleven. I kept workin' construction or landscaping jobs, with a bit of weed dealing on the side, and she worked at Timmy's or other coffee places.

We broke up in Montreal when she met a younger guy and cheated, then left me. As everyone back home says, *What a sin.*

I loved her so much. I would've done anything for her. I got in fights for her, but nothin' serious.

Nicki doesn't even like hearing Heather's name, so we don't talk about her. I'm not in touch with her much anyway. But it makes Nicki crazy when she calls or texts.

I know how that is, even though I make a point to never show it.

Before I met Nicki, I never dated anyone so worldly. I'm pretty sure that one day she'll wake up and wonder what the hell she's doin' with me. I still want to live the fantasy as long as I can.

Dez

The first time I saw her, I noticed how light she was on her feet. She was tall, almost my height, and seriously lean.

Her feet did this skipping thing across the room, flip-flopping soundlessly. She was wearing this tight skirt, and the first thing I noticed were her tanned legs, her thin but delicately defined calves. She had a tank top on that showed off her arms and shoulders. There was too much muscle definition for her to call it good genes, or natural anything. She looked like one of those girls who lived at the gym, drank protein shakes and only ate salads.

She had nice lips, perfectly bow-shaped like a cartoon character. She wore no makeup. She had sea-grey eyes. When she started speaking, I tried to place her accent.

Are you Scottish, I asked her eventually.

She laughed. *I'm South African*, she said.

I had a friend from South Africa in Brazil, I told her. *He sounded different to you.*

She nodded. *I'm Afrikaans.*

What kind of language is that? I asked her. *Is it like Swahili?*

She rolled her eyes, and laughed. *No. It comes from Dutch, mixed with a bit of English, maybe a little German, a little French. Mostly Dutch though.*

Is that your background, I asked her.

She nodded. *Some of my family's originally Dutch. Some are Belgian, Flemish. It's a mix.*

How do you pronounce your last name, I asked her, looking at her resumé.

Marlize Van Zyl. The 'v' in Afrikaans is like 'f' in English, the 'z' is like 's'. Fun Sale, she said, *you pronounce it Fun Sale.*

I smiled. *You're funny*, I told her.

I'm serious, she said, but she smiled.

Where are you from in Brazil? Are you from Rio de Janeiro?

I rolled my eyes back at her and laughed. *No, I'm from the southeast, a small city called Belo Horizonte. It means beautiful horizon.* She nodded. *Where are you from in South Africa?*

Cape Town, she said. *Have you been?*

No, but I hear it's beautiful.

Ja, it is, she said. *A lot of crime though.*

Brazil too, I said.

She nodded again. *I've heard.*

We have a lot to talk about, I told her. I asked her how she'd heard of the bar, and why she wanted to work here.

I came here with my roommate last week, and I loved it, she said. *I was happy when I saw your ad. CDRR reminds me of the Independent Armchair, this really rad bar in Observatory in Cape Town.*

What's it like?

Oh, Obs is great. It's full of university students and artists and musicians. There's an anarchist shop and health food shops, and shops that sell crystals and new age stuff. Lots of great bands play at the Armchair. It's very intimate, and laid back, with couches next to the stage. It's kind of like seeing a concert in your living room. She paused. *This place is cooler. It's more edgy.*

I laughed. *Thanks.*

I got up to make some coffee. *Can I make you a little coffee*, I asked her.

Like an espresso?

I laughed a little at myself. *No, just regular coffee*, I said. *For some reason, in Brazil we say* um cafezinho, *a little one, even though we usually mean a huge cup.*

That's cute, she said.

I asked her what shifts she wanted, what hours she could work, and told her what the job involved. I felt a little protective and asked her if she knew what this neighbourhood was like at night.

You could be working late shifts, I said, *and walking around here on your own.*

She laughed. *Please*, she said, *it's nothing compared to what I've seen.*

She said the job sounded good, and I gave it to her. She was jumpy, I remember that too. I reached out to touch her shoulder, her arm; her skin looked so tawny and smooth. She flinched, and I was surprised. It was the kind of foolproof hitting-on-a-girl-but-not-hitting-on-her thing that almost always worked. *Maybe she was the kind of girl that made you work for it,* I remember thinking. I remember wondering if she did yoga too. She looked flexible.

I told her she could start the next day. She flashed me a huge smile. She glided over to me, shook my hand, held on a few extra seconds. I gave her hand a squeeze. Her arm was shaking a little. She was nervous, I realized. On her way out, she looked back at me, and held my gaze for at least a minute or two before she kept walking. That's what I remember the most: that last look, that lingering that didn't mean to linger, that knew better but couldn't help itself.

There's something about her, I remember thinking, *a little mysterious, a little different.*

I tried to absorb the feeling for as long as I could before I went back to work.

I tried not to think about it. Feelings throw everything off.

Lukas

Nicki asks me to go with her to a work lunch at CDRR. It's like staff appreciation or something because they been doin' really good business. It's Thanksgiving and I really don't wanna go. It's weird bein' in Toronto so far away from the people I love. They offer me time and a half at work, but I'm too depressed to go in.

I work at a bar, remember, she says, smilin'. *We'll get free beer, and free food. My boss is going to get the cooks to make Brazilian food.* She's all excited. *Plus you'll get to meet everyone.*

I nod. *Yeah, okay,* I say. *But don't get mad if I get drunk as fuck if it goes on for hours.*

She laughs. *Hopefully we'll all get drunk if it goes on for hours.*

I kiss her neck. *Let's just stay in,* I beg. I kiss her collarbones. I start unbuttoning her shirt.

She moans then moves away. *I'd love to, but I can't,* she says.

What is Brazilian food anyway, I ask her.

I don't have a clue, she says, *but I think they eat a lot of meat.*

We get there at noon. It's dark inside, and you can just see the looks on the staff's faces, askin' themselves what the hell they're doin' at work on their day off.

Nicki sits down at a table with four other waitresses.

The skinniest one introduces herself as Marlize.

I realize I hooked up with the one at the end of the table a couple months before I met Nicki. She had long blonde hair, and wore a low cut t-shirt. She invited me upstairs when her shift was over.

I fucked her in the bathroom, but when I offered to call her the next day, she said, *Don't.*

She said her name was Ashley, I think.

I avoid making eye contact. I hold Nicki's hand and introduce myself to all of them as her boyfriend.

We sit down and Dez walks right over to us.

Hey man, what're you sayin'? I ask, and he looks at me all funny.

I wasn't saying anything, he says, and it dawns on me that I'm surrounded by foreigners.

I laugh. *It just means how are ya*, I say. *It's something we say on the east coast.* I look at him again. *How's it goin'?*

Oh, I'm good, man. He looks around. *Is so great to have everyone here.*

Have some chopp, he says, and hands me a bottle of beer with German writing on the label. He pours Nicki a *caipirinha*, which she says tastes like lime and sugar.

We start to relax and talk shit.

They serve us liver with onions, some type of spicy sausage, fried eggplant and barbecued pork. It's delicious, but it's weird not havin' any turkey.

They all start talkin' about Thanksgiving, goin' around the tables talkin' about all the shit they're grateful for this year. I start thinkin' about people back home and it feels like someone's standing on my windpipe.

I get up and tell them I gotta go to the bathroom.

I notice framed art for sale on the hallway walls upstairs. There's a pen drawing called "Dogface" by some local artist, and two landscape photos of Queen Street by Nicki. One's of graffiti just outside our apartment. I'm surprised she didn't tell me.

The unisex bathroom walls are covered in graffiti words and drawings. There's even a jar full of different-coloured sharpies. Above the urinal are the words *Radical Feminism or Death.* In smaller letters underneath, someone else has written, *Or you know, just, equality in general.* I roll my eyes. They're still talkin' about Thanksgiving when I get back.

Have you guys seen what's on the walls in the bathroom? All this feminist shit. It's so funny.

Dez smiles. *I love that our clientele is so intelligent,* he says. *I wouldn't be surprised if it was men who wrote some of that stuff.*

I can't believe this guy. Nicki's always sayin' what a player he is. Dez starts tellin' this story about how his mom had feminist books in the house, and how he stole her copy of *The*

Second Sex when he was fourteen, 'cause he thought it was a dirty book. They all laugh. I have no fuckin' idea what's so funny.

I love Simone de Beauvoir, Nicki says.

Marlize starts talkin' about South African feminist writers.

Dez talks about booking some events, like spoken word poetry, or female punk bands.

They both look at him all dreamy, and I wanna hurl. I get up to get myself another beer. I stand at the bar for a while, tryin' to figure out what to do. Nicki comes up to me after what feels like an hour.

I'm having so much fun, she says, slipping her arm around my waist. *Are you?*

No, I say, *I'm not. It's four o'clock now.* She nods. *I think it's time go.*

Okay, she says. She drags her feet like a four-year-old being forced to go to bed early. She wants to say goodbye to Dez on her way out. He's deep in conversation with Marlize who's laughin' really loudly. She must be tanked.

Have a good day man, I say, as Nicki tries to find her jacket.

Happy Thanksgiving, Dez yells back, and I have to run outside to get away from all of them.

Dez

My staff lunch is a success. It's 7:00 p.m. and four of them are still here.

I don't want to make them clean up on their day off, so I tell them to go home. *Get out of here*, I say, *the night's still young.*

I start sweeping the floor.

Marlize is sitting on a barstool, her toned legs dangling off the edge.

She's drinking what must be her tenth *cachaça*. Her cheeks are flushed and her arms are resting loosely on the ledge. She looks beautifully relaxed.

Don't you want to go home? I ask her. She shrugs.

Not really, hey, she answers. *My roommate's having all these friends, and I just don't feel like being around them.*

I nod. *How do you and your roommate know each other?*

We're in the same program at university. She advertised on a bulletin board.

She gets up and brings the mop and bucket from the back room.

Thanks, I say. She nods. *Do you like her?*

She's okay. She always wants to talk too much. She asks me millions of questions about South Africa, and my life there. I never want to talk about it, you know?

I nod. *Of course, you're here now.*

She smiles.

Where do you guys live anyway? I ask.

Queen and John. Do you know Stephanie Street?

You live in that big concrete building? The one beside Grange Park?

She nods.

I think of the dealers who come through here who work in that area. I suddenly feel protective. *Be careful walking through that park at night,* I say.

Please, man, she says, grinning. *I could walk through that park naked at 2 a.m., and nothing would happen to me.*

I laugh and try to force that image out of my head.

Let me give you a ride home, I offer.

She nods. *Okay.*

We get into the car, and I ask if I can play some Brazilian music. I put on my favourite band, Ovos Presley.

Her eyes widen. *This is not what I expected*, she says. *What genre is this?*

I laugh. *It's called psychobilly punk. What were you expecting, bossa nova?*

I have no idea, she says, laughing. *I've never heard bossa nova. I actually like this. Do you have Thanksgiving in Brazil?*

We do. It's called Dia de Ação de Graças. *It's a religious holiday, you know, thanking the Almighty for our blessings and all that. We do it in November. Do you have it in South Africa?*

She shakes her head.

For some reason I don't think we got to her turn at the bar. I ask, *What are you thankful for, Marlize?*

She looks down at her hands. *I'm thankful to live in a safer place*, she says quietly.

Uai, the crime, I ask her. She nods, her face darkening.

I'm thankful for that too, I say, and she looks at me.

I'm thankful to be alive, she says, and I nod.

Yeah, I say, thinking out loud, *aren't we all.*

When we get to her driveway, she invites me to come upstairs. *Come have some tea*, she says.

I don't think it's a good idea, I say.

For a second, I think I see a flicker of disappointment in her eyes. *Okay then, I'll see you tomorrow*, she says a little coldly.

I pull her into a hug. *Thanks for staying later with me today. Thanks for helping. I'd love to hang out with you more, you know, when you're feeling less tipsy.*

She laughs. *I don't usually get drunk. I like to drink, but I usually know when it's enough.*

I wave my hand. *It's not a big deal. It happens to everyone sometimes.*

I give her a kiss on the cheek before she gets out of my car.

I'll come over on a different day, I promise her, and I find myself wondering if I mean it.

Lukas

When I was sixteen, I got in a fight with this greasy fuckin' bastard who hit on my girlfriend every single time he saw her. One night we were all hangin' out at my buddy John's house. We were all drunk as fuck, and this dickshit just walked right up to her, and squeezed her tits. She was pregnant with my kid, and I just fuckin' lost it. She wasn't showing or anything, but she only had one beer so he could've figured it out. Cheryl loved to drink. I heard her tellin' him to fuck right off, but he kept ignoring her. She was freaked out, thinkin' he was gonna try to rape her. I saw this look of real fear in her eyes and I wanted to fuckin' smear his blood all over the room.

I was shakin' when I went over to him, so angry I was even scarin' myself. I grabbed him by the scruff of his neck, I threw the first punch, got the motherfucker right on the chin, and he hit me back, but he was drunker than me so he missed. I'd never had a fight that was so full on—we were kicking and yelling, rolling on the floor and hitting each other. He bit me at some point, but I fought harder, punched and kicked him everywhere til I heard something crack. I was bleedin' places and so was he, but he let out this scream that sounded like a pig being slaughtered.

Something inside me went very cold, and for a second I thought maybe how serious it was. He couldn't get up, couldn't move.

Cheryl was screamin', *Oh my god, what did you do, Luke, what the fuck did you do?*

Everything felt hysterical and suspended, like our lives were part of a set on a bad TV show and we were just standin' there, all foolish watchin' it.

Let's get the fuck out of here, she said, cryin', rubbin' snot and tears and mascara on my shoulder.

John said he'd call 911. *Things'll be okay, bro, just chill the fuck out, go home, get cleaned up.*

I just knew they wouldn't be.

You just get that feeling sometimes that you've gone way too far.

I got the call the next day. I'd broken shit in the guy's back, and a bunch of witnesses seen it. My high school friends were all in line to sell me out. The guy'd be in a wheelchair, a paraplegic was the word they kept using. He'd never be able to use his legs or lower body again. I could come visit him if I wanted, just to see what I did to him.

The doctors said I'd injured his spinal cord, caused *peripheral nerve trauma* and *nerve compression* to his back. *It's not the kind of damage you can reverse*, they said, all straight talking. *He's going to have leg paralysis, not to mention bladder control problems.*

The doctors also told me he'd broken my collarbone and I'd lost two of my back teeth. I even swallowed one of 'em. I also cracked and chipped my front tooth. I was pretty banged up, bruises and scratches, but still there was no question who was worse off. When it came to the trial, it was obvious who was guilty.

I had a court-appointed lawyer, a youngish dude, who kept tellin' me that the *Youth Criminal Justice Act* was there to protect me.

Don't worry, he said. *You're still under eighteen. They won't put your name in the paper, or your picture in the media. No one will know it was you. This will all blow over.*

Some stupid part of me didn't want it to just blow over. I wanted to be punished, fried like popcorn shrimp in an electric chair in Texas, or hung until my eyes popped out of my head while everyone who knew me shook their heads and walked away. I wanted to die.

Nothin' could take away the guilt I'd have to walk around with forever.

It didn't matter when Cheryl testified that she'd been scared for her life. It didn't matter she swore I protected her from rape, or being shoved so hard she could've lost our baby.

There are other ways to handle these things, son, the judge said flatly.

Yeah, well you fuckin' tell me how, motherfucker, I wanted to scream, but I kept my mouth shut.

I was sentenced to two years in juvie, and slapped with adult assault charges. I got a criminal record, and if I broke the law again, even if I didn't pay a parking ticket, or jaywalked in front of a cop, it'd be fuckin' off to jail to do hard time.

Cheryl and I broke up and I lost custody of my kid. She turned against me big time when I lost the trial. Once in a while they'd send me a postcard or a letter. They're still in the Valley, livin' in a trailer in New Minas. I send them money two or three times a year.

He'd be eight now, my little guy. I don't even know if he'd recognize me if he saw me, or if he'd even wanna talk to me. His name's James, after my real dad, who died when I was young. I wanted to call him Jimmy, but she calls him Jamie.

I never told Nicki nothin' about any of this.

Cheryl sent me some school photos of Jimmy, I mean Jamie, a month ago, and I told Nicki he was my nephew. I couldn't believe how big he'd gotten. My eyes were gettin' wet, so I just made up some bullshit about how much I missed my family back home. I couldn't tell her, right? She said it was sweet that I was being so sensitive.

Another fucked up thing is, I can't ever leave Canada. All Nicki ever talks about is travellin'. I try to convince her that there's a lot to see in Canada—we can take a road trip, rent a car, actually see the Rockies out west, or the ocean out east, but she wants to see the world. I forget half the places she wants to see, but I remember Fiji, Barbados, Sweden and New Zealand. She tries to reassure me that I shouldn't be afraid to travel, as if that's the problem. It's a fucking joke.

I'm a felon, I want to yell, but I don't. I just bullshit her about a fear of flyin'.

Nicki's really sweet and weirdly innocent. How can she ever understand? She deserves so much better than me. I like comin' home to her sometimes, exhausted, talkin', fuckin', laughin'. It's nice she's always there. I don't deserve it, obviously, but I can't give her up.

I know it'd be better if I wasn't so goddamn selfish.

Marlize

It's late, 2:30 a.m. We're getting ready to close up. I've cleaned, straightened up the bar, put all the glasses and stray cutlery in the dishwasher. I've wiped down all the tables and menus, put them away, swept and mopped the floors. Dez has taken out the trash, three exploding bags, written in the shifts for the next few days, restocked the bottles behind the bar from the backroom.

We're done. *I'm finished,* I say, and sigh, but he seems amped.

He pulls out a chair for me at the table nearest the bar, produces a bottle of vintage Merlot and two clean glasses. I wonder if it'll be as good as Stellenbosch wine. The cheapest wine from the Cape is still better than anything I've ever had here.

He pours me a glass. *Sit, girl you've earned it,* he says. *I saw you, killing it with the customers tonight.*

I take a sip. I find myself smiling. *This is quite good, hey.* I pat my pocket. *They were lank generous tonight.*

Nah, it was you, you were great, he says. *You deserve all of it.* He reaches for my hand across the table, takes it gently. He catches me off guard, like always. I pull away before I realize what I'm doing.

It's okay, he tells me, says it softly, the way you talk to a little kid. *I'm not going to bite you*—he pauses and looks me in the eye—*unless you're into that.*

I laugh, then look away.

You okay? he asks me, his voice full of concern.

I don't say anything. I don't trust myself to answer. I shake my head, wave my hand as if to brush off his question. I try to apologize with my eyes. His niceness always throws me off. He's the kind of guy who's always surrounded by hot girls, who has the reputation of sleeping with anyone, but then he says genuine things, and I'm confused. Could he actually like me?

Is he wild because he just hasn't met the right woman yet? He must be thirty-one or thirty-two, around ten years older than me. Is he even capable of committing to someone? I'm not sure I want to try.

The other thing that surprises me about Dez is his intelligence. He's not intellectual like the people at university who use words like *hegemony* and *paradigm* in every conversation, but he's clever with people, clever in how he handles situations. He breaks up arguments in the bar with one or two words, calms down angry customers in two seconds. He's articulate and gives fast, funny comebacks. He's also beautiful. His eyes shine like onyxes glinting in the sun. He always looks like he just rolled out of bed, like it's all effortless, man, without actually looking dirty or messy. I don't know how he does it. Sometimes I want to reach out and play with his hair. I control the urge by pretending there's sticky tape on the inside of my hands.

Everyone at work constantly gossips about him, about who he's doing that day, or hour, or week. It'd be hard not to know what he's like, even if I wasn't interested. I'm not sure I want to be someone he doesn't even remember sleeping with him.

We drink more and more though, and talk more. He tells me he's lonely, and I slap his arm.

Ag, please, I say. I'm getting tipsy now. *Give me a break.*

He pulls out a second bottle. He tells me he doesn't even remember how many girls he's been with. *More than two hundred probably.* He tells me how afraid he was to get tested.

He thought he was always safe but wasn't sure. When he found out that he was STD free, and most importantly, AIDS and HIV free, he wanted to throw a party. He sighs. *How pathetic is that,* he asks me.

No, I say, *it's really not. I know what you mean.*

He laughs. *Seriously,* I say, stare at him.

His eyes widen.

Why do you think I'm here, I ask him. *I mean, here, in Toronto.*

I take a deep breath, and a huge gulp of wine, finish what's in my glass before I say anything else.

I was raped in the house I grew up in, in front of my dad, on a Sunday night, I blurt out. *Three guys broke in. My mom and sister were killed when they came home unexpectedly. The police never caught them, but they never catch anyone there. Anyway, my dad and my grandparents paid for me to come study here. They wanted me to get out of the country. It's weird, my life is weird. Nothing like how I imagined it would be two years ago. But I know what you mean, I really do. In South Africa, the crime is like the lottery. You never know who's going to be hit, and why. The AIDS rates are very high. They call it the slow puncture. I thought for sure I'd end up getting it from that night, and I think a part of me wished for it after everything I went through, but I didn't. I don't have it for some reason. I was really, really lucky.*

I stop to breathe, suck in air, stare at the dirty walls full of staples and ripped posters for music events, the now shiny floor, anywhere but at him.

He is quiet for what feels like an hour. I don't know what to do. I start to get up but he stops me.

I'm sorry, he says, *I'm so sorry, I didn't know.*

Of course, I say. *Of course you didn't, man. How could you?*

I'm so sorry, he says again. Then—*You're so strong.*

I smile a little, a tiny bit.

Then—*It's not your fault.*

I nod. I know.

Then—*God, is just so terrible, is so unfair, Marlize, God, so terrible, I'm so sorry. You've been through so much. You're . . . you're so strong.*

He gets up, comes to my side of the table and puts his arms around me. I don't stop him this time.

We stay like that for a while. Then he helps me up, takes me by the hand, leads me to the door. My legs are shaky. He turns off the light, locks up behind me, walks me home.

He puts his arm around me as we get closer to my apartment. *So we both got lucky, we both got so lucky,* he says, and I laugh. He looks at me. *You're doing good, girl,* he says, and gives me a hug.

As we stand in the doorway of my building, shivering, light from the lobby hits his face, and I can see him properly for the first time. His eyes are wet.

I'm so sorry you had to go through that, he says, and puts his arms around me again.

I sigh, breathe in the wine fumes, the cold air. I smile.

I want to tell him how much tonight means to me, and how happy I am that he's listened to me talk about something I've kept inside for so long, but I don't know how.

Maybe one day I will tell him.

Nicki

I know it's going to snow this morning. I can smell it.

The air has this heavy dampness about it. It's the twenty-second of December, and everyone at work keeps saying they want it to be a white Christmas.

I never experienced real winter until I moved here, and I hate the deep coldness in my bones, but there's something magical about snowfalls.

I stand outside and breathe in deep as if the smog and smoke are good for me.

I go inside to watch, and wait, watch the ground get lightly dusted with sparkling icing sugar. Watch the neighbours shovel their driveways until they build knee-high hills on the sidewalk. Watch the cars drive by spraying water and dirt and mud, turning it into brown and grey slush.

Watch people slip and slide, fall in mid conversation, mid cell phone call, face plant. Try not to laugh. It will happen to me, when I leave the house one night, when it's too dark to see, or during the day, when there's black ice, it will happen to me, I know. I refuse to buy those ugly winter boots that everyone wears here. I love to watch the winter from the inside.

People come home from work early and want to go out less. Lukas complains that he's bored, but there's a calmness to it. I teach him how to play backgammon, which we call *shesh besh* in Israel, and he teaches me card games. We drink cheap wine, and watch *Seinfeld* reruns or bad TV movies and talk about work. Mainly I talk, and he listens. Sometimes he makes fun of people. I tell him I think Dez has a crush on Marlize.

Ugh, Dez is such a sleaze, he says, making a face. *I don't know how you can work for him.*

He's kind of fun, I say. *He's funny. He's over the top like those actors in Spanish Telenovellas.*

But he doesn't even try to hide it. Lukas is visibly angry. *You got good morals, Nicki. I think you should just stay away from him.*

I shrug. *What's wrong with being open about who you are? At least he's honest.*

He is quiet for about five minutes.

Anyway, good for Marlize, he says after another minute. *Maybe she'll stop being such a bitch to you if she's finally getting laid.*

I shrug. *Maybe,* I say.

I tell him about the guy at the bar who kept asking me where I was from, insisting on knowing. I never say, I just ask people where they think I'm from, and agree with whatever they say. It's easier. I've travelled a lot, so I can usually bullshit my way through a conversation about most places.

For some reason, two nights ago, I decided to tell the truth.

The guy had long brown dreads with wooden beads in them. He reminded me of the kind of guys we have back home who travel to India after their time in the army, the kind who are laid back and smoke lots of weed, and are generally fun to be around. We'd describe him as *shanti.* He was sitting on his own, with a backpack, drinking glass after glass of blond on tap. He was friendly.

I said I was from Israel, and it turned into a whole big thing, all the stuff I'd spent my life trying to avoid.

He told me he was from Nova Scotia.

Plenty of idiots where I'm from, believe me, I remember Lukas telling me once.

The guy started talking, gently at first, and then more and more angrily about how he'd read about Gaza, how it was a sin, what was happening there.

I didn't know what to say. I was careful. I said, *It's true, people are suffering for no reason, it's wrong,* which was what I really did think.

He started bringing up the army, slurring, talking about how people, including girls, are forced to go, and did I go.

What does it matter, I asked him, but he insisted that it did, so, *Yes,* I said, *yes, fine, I did go. I sat at a desk, in an office in an army base doing things I'm still not allowed to talk about. I was in Intelligence. I had to.*

It sounds pretty easy, he said.

You don't know the half of it, I said. *I did basic training, learned how to fire a gun, how to randomly hate and fear strangers. They tried to indoctrinate me. I felt like I couldn't leave, like I didn't have a choice.* Some people I knew pretended to be crazy, dropped acid before their army interviews, said they heard voices, feared planes crashing into their bedroom windows.

I didn't have the guts to do that though. My parents put fear into me about a psychiatrist's file following me through life, a big red stamp that said *crazy* all over any work file, or official profile about me.

I didn't have the guts to not do what everyone else I knew was doing. I couldn't leave before, so I left after. I might never go back, but I still didn't know where I wanted to be.

So what's your real name? It's not really Nicki is it? He tried to grab my hand.

It's Nili, actually, I said. *But I prefer Nicki. And I'm not interested.*

You should be who you are, dude, he said, smacking into a wall on the way out.

I don't understand what's wrong with being whoever I want to be, especially when it feels truer sometimes than who people think I actually am.

Marlize

I didn't get my period until I was seventeen. It was different from my friends at school, but exactly like my friends who were dancers. Becoming a member of a dance company when I graduated from high school was all I let myself think about. Being really thin, maintaining a weight low enough to move gracefully, to be lifted and twirled by a male dancer, for the costumes to hang loosely and fit just right, was part of the job description.

We smoked, we restricted our diets and *kotched* into toilets or bins when we knew we ate too much. We all covered for each other constantly.

We congratulated each other on our flat breasts, cracked heels and bleeding toes.

The joy I felt when I glided across the studio dance floor, or when I spun across the stage, unable to feel my own weight, was just better. The victories were just better than the sacrifices.

When people were watching you, when an audience was staring, mesmerized by a beauty that you helped to create, just by working hard and participating, it was the best feeling in the world.

I danced two kinds of ballet—classical and contemporary. Classical was the more difficult of the two—a lot of pointe work, standing on the tips of your toes in special shoes that turn out your legs away from the body. Lots of high extensions. It always had to look graceful, flowing and precise. Even if your muscles were killing you, you had to make it look ethereal.

My teachers taught the Russian Vaganova method, which meant lots of dramatic turns, tricky *grande jetés* and intricate *pas de chats* that looked like they were defying the laws of gravity. My daydreams were always of being in a performance with that perfect moment where I would appear to be hovering in midair.

I always had to remember the names, and precise techniques, of each movement. I always had to exercise—strengthening my lower body, my legs, my core. I constantly thought about increasing my flexibility, having stronger muscles.

Contemporary ballet combined classical with modern. You still did pointe work, but there was a greater range of movement. It felt more innovative to me. When I danced contemporary, I felt more alive. I think it was also more fun for the audience to watch. The music and outfits were more colourful and decorated, and you saw more joy in each movement.

Dancing let me own my body. It made every muscle and every movement voluntary, and a conscious decision. It always helped me to connect and feel in touch with myself.

I'd see people at school treating their bodies so disrespectfully: pouring rubbish into themselves—chocolate, chips, *biltong*—and I'd feel disgusted.

They didn't understand my dedication to it—the five hours a day I'd spend practising during the week, the eight hours a day I'd spend dancing on Saturdays.

My sister didn't understand it at all. When she came home from university she'd tell us stories, full of excitement, about her friends, and her classes, and the parties she went to.

I told her that her life sounded great, but it was totally foreign to me. I didn't tell my sister that it sounded empty. That it seemed like she was searching for meaning, and a sense of community that I'd already found. I knew I was lucky. I didn't know how to express it, but I knew that I was.

My mother worried about me all the time. She was always *hakking* me that I was too thin, pestering me night and day to eat more, to eat anything.

When I was fifteen, I learned how to make it look like I was eating more. I'd move my food around, chew at least twenty times before swallowing, and keep a serviette on my lap to spit into when she wasn't looking.

My mom didn't really understand either—it wasn't about a clothing size or worrying that boys didn't like me. It was purely about movement. It was about the size of my dreams versus the size of my frame. I was comfortable with my decisions. But still, I didn't want her to worry about me. When I was sixteen, I pretended to get my period. My mother was threatening to take me to the doctor, get my hormones tested. She was worried that I was never going to be able to have children.

I was in the bathroom at school, playing with a cuticle on my index finger, as I washed my hands. It bled more than I expected, down my finger, into my palm and onto my wrist. I grabbed a piece of toilet paper to dab it with, until it occurred to me what I could be doing with the blood instead. I asked another girl, who was washing her hands in the next sink, if she had an extra pad. I locked myself in a stall, ripped the skin on my finger a little more, stuck the pad to my underwear, and let the extra blood fall onto it. I hardly felt anything.

I didn't think my mother would ask to see the pad, but I wanted to have evidence to show her in case she did.

I knew that she didn't always understand everything I did, but I always felt how much my mother loved me. I never wanted to do anything that hurt her—and we both knew that my not getting my period was by my own design. Periods caused bloating, and hormone changes and weight gain. I just couldn't risk it. I thought that I would've done anything to protect my mom from being hurt. I didn't know how far she'd be willing to go to protect me one day.

Lukas

Jerks get cancer, too. That's the first thing I hear gettin' into work this morning. Two nurses from the ICU are talkin' about this young guy who has terminal cancer. They're sayin' he's a prick, yellin' at them, throwin' shit and treatin' them and the family who visits him like he wishes they'd just leave him alone.

The one nurse says, *Hey, if you were twenty-two, and you knew you were dying, you'd be angry too.*

The other nurse shakes her head. *Maybe it's the cancer, but maybe that was what he was like before.*

It can happen to anyone.

I can't think about anything else for hours.

I work five or six days a week, every day or night. I either work the morning shift, from 7 a.m. to 3 p.m., or the evening, from 9 p.m. to 5 a.m.

There are twelve floors, full of what the nurses call *soothing* colours, like beige, light blue, avocado green, and puke yellow, and, like they love to tell the patients, lotsa natural light.

I don't have any specific route; sometimes I'm in emergency, or burn wards, or operating rooms, or ICU or terminal illnesses. If I'm really unlucky, I spend a day on a garbage run, runnin' between the elevators and the garbage room, or in the psych wards.

I start every day with a checklist. I have to make sure I have a whole cart full of supplies—mop heads, broom heads, long broom sticks, disinfectant wipes, gloves, garbage bags, rolls of paper towel, toilet paper.

I share a janitor's closet with a woman named Betty, who's probably older than my mother. I don't see her often, because we work opposite shifts. The locker is decorated with thank-you cards from the nurses, drawings from her grandchildren. There are two "Get Well Soon" balloons in silver and red taped to the ceiling. It's strangely comforting.

My first job of the day is to go to the nurse's station and sign out my keys. For the first two or three hours, I try to keep my head down—do my job without makin' any small talk. I get peanut butter cups or Oh Henry! bars from the vending machine, make crappy coffee, then clean up the kitchenette, start takin' out the garbage bags on my floor. They say the bags aren't supposed to be filled with medical waste, or sharps, but I've pricked myself, through my gloves, at least five or six times since I been here.

I go into the rooms on my floor, make beds, clean surfaces, doorknobs, counters. The bathrooms are always the most disgusting—garbage bags full of adult diapers and used tampons. I try not to breathe it in. A couple days ago I had to clean a bathroom that had diarrhoea everywhere—like someone took a shit in a bucket and threw it around. It was all over the walls, the floor, the door, the mirror, the sink. Only a tiny bit actually made it into the toilet. I can't imagine how it happened, the angles, the speed, the way the guy had to stand to get it all over like that. Did he put his back against the door, lift his hands, and explode?

And how are you supposed to begin to clean something like that up? Are you supposed to use a shovel? A rag, a mop? Where do you even put it? Just fuckin' damaged, man!

The easiest, cleanest place to work is the burn ward. The beds are super-cushioned, and the surfaces are softer. The patients' faces and arms are covered in bandages, and they're doped up beyond belief. It feels awkward, you want to talk to them, but you don't know what to say. It's like walkin' up to a car accident, seein' a person lying there on the ground, wanting to help 'em, but all you can do is sweep up the glass around them.

The ER is where you see people in the most immediate pain—little kids who jumped off the roof thinkin' they could fly, teenagers doin' stupid shit when they're drunk, the ones in gangs who just got shot or stabbed, arms and legs and hips twisted and dislocated, limbs that look like they might fall off. You just work around them, try not to make eye contact, or do anything that would cause any more hysteria.

But it's definitely weird.

Only once so far did I have to help clean the OR. In the off hours, they take dead bodies there to be harvested for organs. There's a machine that goes up and down the body, removing thin pieces of skin, the top layer. It looks like marble underneath, bright red with thin swirls, like distorted carpet burn. I've watched it take bodies apart. I'm always fascinated, until my guilt pulls me away. It isn't part of my job, just my own entertainment. I've been so mesmerized, it didn't even register that I was lookin' at a dead person.

The psych ward is definitely the worst place. The rooms are easy to clean—they have nothin' in them, because anything can be used by patients to harm themselves. There are silent rooms, where people sit around and you're not allowed to say anything to them. They walk around like zombies, with glassy eyes that don't focus on you when you look at 'em. They look like their souls been ripped right outta them. There's something about them, even the mildest cases, that look different to people you see on the subway or on the street.

There's this one guy, Terry, who's violent, screamin', frothin' at the mouth. I walk past his room, and hear him bangin' his fists as hard as he can against the walls. When I walk past, he swears, and lunges at the door. Every time I have to clean his room and he doesn't beat the crap outta me I feel grateful.

It fucks me up, havin' to work there. Sometimes, I don't go home. I stay over at my friend Mike's house, talk shit, drink or smoke a bowl, watch movies or TV.

Sometimes I can't handle how intense Nicki is. I don't want to talk about my day in detail, and I don't have the patience to hear about hers. I can't even meet her at the end of her shift if we happen to end at the same late time anymore. I just wanna do nothin', you know? Pretend the whole day or even the week didn't happen.

Nicki seems cool, though, most of the time.

She accepts that on some nights, we just need our own space.

Nicki

Basic training, or what we call *tironut,* in the army was a nightmare. I always laughed when I saw exercise classes in North American gyms being described as "boot camp." Please, they had no idea what boot camp really was.

I remembered it being a total shock to the system, exhilarating and terrifying. The first few days were a blur of discipline, countless push-ups and running as punishment for talking and laughing, being barked at by drill instructors for not understanding commands, for not catching on fast enough. On my second week in, I got caught smoking and talking to a friend when I was supposed to be studying and practising first aid. I got punished with a detention—instead of being allowed to go home that weekend, I was forced to stay at the base on my own. I'd never been so bored in my life.

The only thing that got me through the whole experience was the social part of it—bonding with other girls from all over the country over how hard it was, what we believed in, what we wanted to do when we got out, which boys we thought were cute and how we were going to approach them. My friends got me through it and most of us were still in touch.

In basic training we were certified to fire rifles, drilled on Israeli military history and victories, and made to understand how important our role was in protecting our country. We were taught about how much of the country's budget was spent on the military, and in the end we felt important, a part of the national priority. They told us that we were the best and the brightest, a group strong and powerful enough to be entrusted with an all-important task. By the time we were finished, the indoctrination was supposed to be complete. We were sworn in to the Israeli Defense Forces, received our beret corps certification and went on to more specific training.

There was also a distance-breaking ceremony, where we finally learned the names of our commanders. Since we were about to have different commanders anyway, we were finally allowed to call our old commanders by their first names.

In Israel how well you did in the army, how highly your commander thought of you at the end of your two or three years, was incredibly important to your future. Every job you ever applied for asked for your *Te'udat Zehut*, your national identity number, and your number from when you were in the army. You always had to list your commanding officer as a reference and they would call him or her to find out what kind of worker you were—were you industrious, did you take initiative, did you follow commands well? People who didn't end up in the army for health, or mental health or religious reasons were often seen by potential employers as suspicious, less committed.

I got a good review from my commander but I hated using her as a reference. I had always wanted her to get to know me as a person instead of as a functioning part of the unit. After two years, five bomb blasts or *piguim*—that killed about fifty people in total, and injured hundreds— four deaths of close friends, and the impersonal nature of all of it, I was sure of one thing—I was ready to get the fuck out of Israel. I didn't know where I wanted to go exactly, but I knew I needed to leave.

Marlize

My dad got married in the same purple suit that he buried my Oma in.

He got married three months after my grandmother committed suicide.

They'd been planning the wedding for months. My mom bought a white flowing dress with a thick purple ribbon around the waist. They'd booked the church. Her family was involved with the planning, but Dad hadn't told his parents he was getting married because he hated his father.

My grandparents lived in Vrede, a *dorpie*, or small town in the northeastern Free State. Vrede was full of farms, Dutch Reformed Churches, Boer memorials like the Great Trek monument and the annual *Rooivleisvees*, the red meat festival.

My grandmother's parents had been farmers, but my grandfather worked in mining, as a supervisor.

South Africa produces the most gold in the world, he used to tell us, *and the Free State is the biggest in the country*.

He'd travel to mines in places like Sasolburg and leave his family on their own for days or even weeks at a time. When he wasn't working, and he was home, he'd drink and beat my grandmother. My dad was an only child, and the older he got, the less my grandparents bothered to hide it from him.

When he was eighteen, my dad moved to Cape Town.

He was accepted to UCT where he studied and met my mom. He got a job in advertising when he graduated and after a year he asked my mom to marry him. They decided to get married up the west coast on the white sand beach of Yzerfontein. They planned to move to the northern suburbs and have kids. He had almost outrun his past.

One day when he was at work, he got the phone call. He was writing the copy for a diet soft drink when my mom told him. My Oma had hung herself. She'd been found swinging from the pipes in their storage room, with one of my Opa's ties around her neck. Their dog was lying at her feet. When they tried to move her, he bared his teeth and tried to attack. He had to be injected with a sedative.

When my parents arrived at my grandparents', my dad was shaking so much that my mother had to practically hold him up to keep him standing. It was the smell, he told me later, of milk left out overnight, of alcohol and sweat and salt.

My Opa was lying prostrate on the couch, face red, hysterical, crying and ranting, while everyone looked on. No one said anything, but it was clear that everyone blamed him.

He wasn't invited to the wedding, and I only saw him a handful of times before he died in 1993.

My mother maintained that he was still my dad's father, still Claudette's and my grandfather.

Ag, Inge, asseblief, my dad would say to her. *Inge, please. They hadn't slept together since I was about twelve. What do you think all his business dinners were about? He treated her like shit. He doesn't deserve our pity.*

I didn't know until my mother died that my own parents hadn't slept together in years either.

I didn't know their problems had been so serious.

I'd been too preoccupied to see the signs of marital decay.

Maybe it was easier, when things didn't feel right, to focus on myself. It was easier to focus on symmetry and my body. Dance made me feel invincible. Dance, unlike people, gave me everything I ever put into it. Dance never disappointed me.

For a long time after I was attacked, I thought about suicide. I thought about going out in a short skirt to a dodgy area in the middle of the night, and waiting for someone to stab me. My dad and I barely spoke, I ignored phone calls and friends, and watched hours of TV. I couldn't even imagine what to do with myself.

I didn't know how I could survive living in a world that I couldn't just glide my way through.

Nicki

My parents call me today from Israel to tell me that my sister is having a baby.

She's four years younger than me and has been married for less than a year.

The conversation is short. My dad talks for two minutes, asks me how I am, if I'm making enough money, what my plans are. My mom starts out friendly but soon is angry, hyperventilating, and screaming.

I do not want to go back for the birth, or if it's a boy, for the *brit milah*, the ceremonial circumcision that happens when the child is eight days old.

My parents owned the penthouse I grew up in, which in Israel, where everyone was in the red, was a sign of tremendous wealth. It could've comfortably housed at least eight.

Our balcony looped all the way around our apartment, and in the summer, when it was thirty-five or thirty-seven degrees during the day, and about thirty at night, I'd fall asleep on one of our loungers, surrounded by white marble floors and walls, staring out at the grass and trees behind the parking lot below, the sounds of neighbours talking, stray cats hissing. We had a stray cat problem on our street, even by Israeli standards.

An old man in my building, he must have been at least eighty, had shrivelled skin hanging on his face, narrow brown eyes, thin strands of remaining grey hair, only two or three visible teeth, wizened hands. He used to collect fish heads, scraps of bread, half containers of yogurt or milk, and he'd feed the cats every single day at 3:00 p.m. Sometimes on Fridays he'd buy them discount cat food at the supermarket on the corner of our street. We had at least twenty of them— fat ginger ones, thin calicos, mangy matted tabbies, ones that were missing eyes, or parts of paws, scratched to shit for stepping on another cat's territory or trying to eat its food.

They slept on or under people's cars, staring at you lazily in the sun, glaring when you made eye contact, daring you to kick them off. My dad hated them—a cat on his windshield in the mornings made him fly into a rage.

Neither of my parents cared much for animals. There was a home video of my dad kicking a cousin's dog as he walked down the aisle at a wedding. My mom didn't want anything that would make the house dirty.

I have enough to do as it is, she would always tell us. *Ein li coakh*, she would say. *I don't have the strength.*

My dad made his fortune in what we call *High Tech* in Israel, but what everyone else in the world calls I.T. He designed software, and created a mapping system for the army to use that they say revolutionized their ability to do tracking. Not only did it give him a reputation for being a genius, it gave him a salary and a title to match, as he loved to tell people. Now he was a boss, telling programmers what to do. He worked for Amdocs, a huge company on the border of my town and the next city. He still worked at least sixty hours a week, so even when I lived at home, I hardly ever saw him.

My mom worked part time in Ramat HaSharon, a suburb of Tel Aviv, as a florist. She liked exotic flowers, oranges and reds and purples, the kind that cost a fortune. Israelis prided themselves on getting a good deal, so it was a hard sell. She'd come home frustrated and complaining, picking me apart, yelling, slamming things. On her days off, she cried and had panic attacks.

My mom did not believe in long-term therapy, or in taking medication.

I'd given up trying to help her but I'd also given up on hearing what a disappointment I was.

My sister Noa was twenty. Her husband, Reuven, was a rabbi. They lived in Bnei Brak, a city full of people so Orthodox they could be the equivalent of America's Amish.

My parents were Modern Orthodox, but they were at least five rungs closer to heaven on the ladder than I was.

They keep Shabbat more or less, and they kept to the laws of being kosher, at least when at home. My mom wore jeans, my dad wore shorts and t-shirts, even to work. Israel was pretty casual compared to Canada.

My sister wore a wig to cover her hair, floor-length denim skirts and long-sleeved shirts even in the summer. She wouldn't sit alone in a room with a man who wasn't her husband, or see a male doctor or dentist, or shake hands with or touch any other man. When they went on vacation, my brother-in-law went to men's-only beaches, and my sister went to women's-only, so they wouldn't be exposed to anyone of the opposite sex.

When she had her period, my sister wasn't allowed to touch her husband in any way, not even accidentally, like if she brushed his arm when she passed him the milk at breakfast. They weren't even allowed to sleep in the same bed at that time, and she had to take a ritual bath once a month, called a *mikvah*, to clean herself.

I didn't want to get involved, but how could I not feel angry when my sister told me about it and then asked me what I thought?

God wants you to hate your body? I asked her. *God wants you to feel uncomfortable and unclean during a time that's totally natural? God wants you to be a leper?*

She shook her head at me. *You don't understand,* she said, looking away, and I guess I didn't.

I guess I didn't even want to.

Her husband, who walked around in a black coat, white shirt, black pants, and a long beard every day, professionally studied commentaries on the Old Testament aside from working in the synagogue, doing rabbi stuff on Friday nights and Saturdays. He went to a *yeshiva*, a place where holy men got together to sit and study the Torah up close, all day. Women couldn't even go inside.

My dad used to call guys like him a drain on our economy—he'd get so angry, claiming his taxes were being spent on supporting people who were too lazy to get real jobs. His favourite example was Rashi, a famous rabbi in Jewish history who wrote biblical commentary.

Even he *had a job as a winemaker*, my dad would snap, banging his hands down on the table as he talked.

Now all he could do was sing Reuven's praises. He was happy to support them, he'd say. They were performing a *mitzvah*, a holy deed. They were continuing the Jewish race, protecting Israelis by increasing our population.

Gotta keep our numbers up, he'd say, and he'd be serious.

How could you argue with that? You couldn't, so I didn't even bother.

Reuven didn't have to go to the army, because *yeshiva* guys like him often get a free pass. Neither did my sister, who did National Service, where she volunteered at a hospital in Jerusalem for a year instead.

I didn't bother to give my opinion on the unfairness of that either. I kept it to myself, in case it actually killed me.

🌍

I started breaking the laws of Shabbat when I was fourteen. I skipped Friday night dinners to go to dance parties in Tel Aviv. I'd lie to my parents and tell them I was staying over at a friend's. When I got my first car, before the army, when I was eighteen, I'd have to park it around the corner on Friday nights or Saturdays so they'd think I walked home from wherever I came from. According to Shabbat laws, any work activity, including driving, was strictly forbidden.

I broke the rules, but I started out small. The first time I did it, I remember expecting a bolt of lightning to shoot out of the sky and kill me, and then, when it didn't, I wanted to test it. I wanted to see how far I could go before God or my parents would smite me, wanted to see how hard I could push. There was no joy in my house growing up and I was determined to find some, somewhere. I'd stumble in on a Friday night, hair smelling like weed, jacket or t-shirt like cigarette smoke, lips and tongue red and wine-soaked.

Nothing bad ever really happened. I got good at tuning out the yelling.

Stoner, my sister used to hiss at me, when I passed her door.

My sister never rebelled, not even once. She never wanted to be anything except a more extreme version of what my parents wanted her to be.

I got my first tattoo after the army. It was a *kivsa shkhora,* a black sheep, on my right hip. I tried to wear it proudly. My first boyfriend came with me to get it. He let me squeeze his hand when the needle went in, and kick his foot every time I thought the pain was too much.

After we broke up I backpacked through Europe for eight months, and ended up in the UK. I was staying with an Israeli friend in a council flat, living on ten-pence instant noodles when my dad called. He offered to pay for a ticket home, and when I said no, he offered to send me to Toronto, to stay with a cousin of his. He thought his cousins could set me straight, but I only lasted two months at Bathurst and Lawrence before moving to Queen Street.

I'm inspired by everything, from the skinny street punks with orange mohawks and hanging chain belts who offer to squeegee my non-existent car, to the phone poles covered in staples and flyers of bands with names like Death on Wheels or Primitive Circus, to the performance artists with silver faces miming for tips, to the street painters selling chalk pastel art on the sidewalks. I love the stores where the windows are filled with rolls of shiny and lacy fabrics and different kinds of buttons that remind me of all the fabric stores on Nachlat Binyamin in Tel Aviv. I finally feel connected to my surroundings and I never want to leave.

Marlize

In the beginning he warns me against being with him.

After we sleep together for the first time he says, *I didn't want to be this guy, I didn't want to do this because I'm fucked up. I'll let you down, I'll say I'll call you but I won't.*

He leans over and traces my lips with the backs of his fingers as he says this. I'm still lying in the bed, covered by my sheets, as he stands by the bed, already dressed. He doesn't sound particularly remorseful, just matter of fact. His voice is soft and playful.

He cracks a small smile, as if to say, *Why do you have to like the guys who fuck you over? Why don't you want to be with a nice guy?*

He doesn't understand: guys who call when they say they will are boring.

I don't want a guy who'll take me to the movies and hold my hand and buy me presents. I've had guys like that. They can still break your heart, there are no guarantees.

I want a guy who knows how to live, the kind of guy who'll expand my horizons instead of making me feel like the world is caving in on me.

I want a guy who'll fuck me, because I'm ready for sex now, ready for it to be fun instead of traumatic.

I want a guy who's not afraid to hurt me, because life is painful, and I'm not afraid.

I just want to really feel, is that too much to ask? I want to live and enjoy and experience because you never know when it will all end.

You don't know what you're getting yourself into, he tells me.

You don't know who you got yourself into, I say, and he thinks about it for two minutes, and then he gets it, and laughs.

You're quick, he says, *I like that,* leans over again and gives me a kiss that's long and full of tongue, that tickles and strokes the backs of my teeth.

I try not to convulse with pleasure. I try, as always, to play it cool.

I won't call you later, he says on his way out. *But I might actually call you tomorrow. I like sexy South African girls who can drink a lot of whiskey.*

A wave of electricity pulses through me. I lie on my back in the bed for hours, thinking about him, trying to wipe the smile off my face. When he calls the next day at 5:00 p.m., I'm surprised. I'd think there'd be more of a chase than this. I can't stop giggling, like a fourteen-year-old with a crush.

It's a short conversation, maybe ten minutes.

What are we going to do about work, he asks me at the end of the conversation. I realize I have no idea.

We spend that night at work with him basically ignoring me, flirting with every girl that walks in, taking phone numbers on balled napkins. One girl even writes hers on his hand. He looks at me and shrugs, like, *I told you, what did you expect.*

I shrug back, like obviously this happened, as if casual sex is like breathing to me.

My disappointment must show on my face. Nicki, who is on shift with me, irritates me with her invasive sympathy.

He's not boyfriend material, she tells me. *I'm saying this because I care. You have eyes, right? He's a waste of your time.*

He excites me, I say. *He makes me feel alive for the first time in ages.*

She looks at me like she's trying to figure me out. *Okay,* she says, *but is it worth it?*

Her relationship, from the looks of it, is boring. Her boyfriend meets her here occasionally at the end of her shift. He looks like the guys I knew who played rugby—tall and broad and not much of a talker. I've tried to make conversation with him once. All I remember is that he said, *Nicki's a good girl*, and put his arm around her protectively.

I know she won't understand.

Look, I tell her, *I'm not on a mission to change him. I just want to have fun in my life sometimes. That's it. Okay?*

She walks away, shaking her head.

I send Dez a text from across the room, knowing he checks it all night. I write: *Going home early. Not feeling well. Seems like you managing okay. Call me if you need anything otherwise see you tomorrow at 6:00.*

He shows up at my door at 3:00 a.m., knocking loudly, waking up my roommate who groans and is furious with me. He seems drunk. He picks me up off the floor and swings me around.

You're not just an employee to me, he says.

No? It actually seemed like it tonight.

See, this is exactly what I told you would happen, and it's happening already, he says.

I sigh. It's true but I don't know if I want him to know it.

I look him in the eye, then look away. I could ask him to leave, and he might do it, but I realize that I don't want him to.

Okay, fine, I say, barely loud enough for him to hear it. *I like you, Dez. I don't know why, but I do.*

He looks at me, shakes his head and smiles. *I like you too, Marlize.*

I start to smile. He sees the expectation creeping into my eyes and he backtracks.

Let's just take it as it comes, okay? Let's just see what happens.

I don't say anything.

Do you think you can do that? Is that okay? Because if it's not, I can go home right now. The last thing I ever want to do is hurt you, baby. I don't want to promise you too much. I really want to be honest with you, Marlize. I care for you.

He looks at me with puppy eyes.

No, I say, *it's okay, come in. It's okay, really.*

I lead him into the living room, onto our couch. We sit whispering so that we don't wake my roommate, until about 5:00 a.m. He tells me a lot about himself, which is more interesting than talking about me. We go to my bedroom, and he tells me he feels close to me. He takes my clothes off gently, kisses me softly, plunges into me as I stand up against my wall.

It feels different than the last time. I try to be quiet, bite into his shoulder, try to hold back screams.

We fall asleep, and he leaves by 10:00. I think we did a great job of keeping it down until I see my roommate later in the day.

She says, *Jesus Christ, if you guys don't learn how to keep it down, I swear to god I'm investing in ear plugs. You're lucky the fucking neighbours didn't hear you.*

I grin like a lottery ticket winner who can't believe her luck. I can't believe having fun could be this easy.

Dez

I was raised so religiously that to this day, my natural impulse is to say a prayer before I sit down to eat.

Abençoai Senhor, a nós e a estes alimentos que vamos receber da vossa bondade. Por Cristo, nosso Senhor. Amém.

Bless us Oh Lord, and these thy gifts, which we are about to receive, from thy bounty, through Christ, Our Lord. Amen.

It has never left me, no matter how much I've wanted it to. That impulse to believe in something, to be grateful, to be thankful and to be afraid of the will of someone else is always there.

My preschool, elementary school, and high school were all-boys, Catholic, and run by priests.

There was an affiliated girl's school that was situated a block away.

I had a good time in high school, since the girls rolled up the waistbands of their skirts the minute the nuns weren't looking, wore large crosses on chains that sat between their breasts, applied makeup, kept lipstick in their bras, and sometimes, if you were good, let you get under their skirts.

Like father, like son, I guess. My dad worked for a pharmaceutical company in town, first as a salesperson and then as a marketing exec. He spent three or four days a week working for the company's biggest branch in Sao Paulo, an eight- or nine-hour drive from where we lived. He had two homes, and whenever I visited him there when I was older, there'd be a slew of girlfriends and mistresses going in and out.

My dad wanted to be the kind of guy that provided for us, who could give us anything we asked for just because we asked. He wanted to be the kind of guy who went to church with us on Sundays and bought my mom flowers for their anniversary. Most of all, I think, he wanted to be my friend. He always wanted to hear about the girls I was with, all the dirty details.

You've got to experience it all while you still can, he would say, *while it's still okay. Voce tem que aproveitar a vida*, he always told me. You have to enjoy your life.

For my eighteenth birthday he even set me up with one of his ex-girlfriends. She met me in his apartment when he was at work. She was ten years older than me, all mouth and slender hands, inky black hair and dusky eyes.

You need to experience a woman, he told me. *Você só vive uma vez.* You only live once.

He played hard, but he worked hard too. He worked sixty or seventy hours a week, easy, and had a heart attack the year he turned fifty. He dropped dead at a conference in Sao Paulo. My mom had some idea of what he'd been up to, but she'd never really wanted to admit it.

They started calling, the ex-girlfriends, one or two of them anyway, saying how sorry they were. My mom broke down for a few days, then became even more religious. She'd walk around clutching rosary beads, praying late at night with my grandmother, never missing a single Sunday service.

I was twenty-one, and angry. I couldn't believe in God anymore, couldn't believe he'd take my dad like that, but I pretended to, for my mom's sake. I went to church with her and my sisters every Sunday. They were both older, married and successful in business. They were both protective of me. When they said I should take a morals and religion course along with my business courses at university that year, I said I'd do it. When they agreed with my mom that I had to find a real woman, a girlfriend to be my wife, instead of all those *galinhas*, slutty girls, I'd been running around with, I went along with it.

I knew as soon as I met Adriana that my mom and sisters would love her. I didn't really think about whether it was right for me, I just knew that I wanted it to be. I wanted to be a good guy, the kind that lived according to the right beliefs. But I also wanted to enjoy my life. I still hadn't figured it out.

If you turn out like your father, my mom told me one day, in tears, *I don't know what I'll do with myself.*

After we got married, Adriana and I left the country, and I was relieved. We went back to visit a couple of times, but my mom never came here. She had no idea how we lived.

When I first moved here, I fantasized about getting a job somewhere on Dundas West and never learning English properly. I knew it would've been easy to open my own *churrascaria*—a Brazilian barbeque restaurant.

It was Adriana who forced me out into the world. *We did not come here*, she said, *to live in a mini Brazil.*

But I don't understand what Canadian culture is, I protested.

She threatened to kick my ass. *We made this huge effort to change our lives, and move here*, she said. *You have to make it work. Get out there and observe what they do here. Make Canadian friends. Try harder.*

It was Adriana who threatened to call my mom in Brazil because I was drinking and partying my inheritance from my dad away. And it was Adriana who suggested I sink my money into something in entertainment, maybe a bar and music hybrid because I'd be successful at what I was passionate about. She encouraged me to create CDRR, to buy the property on Queen, to take the business courses. She was the one who made me believe that I could do it.

I didn't love her, but I owed her something, does that make sense? I couldn't just kick her out of my life no matter how much I sometimes wanted to. Besides, my Catholic mom was strongly against divorce.

For now, we live in different places, split everything down the middle, see each other occasionally. Mostly we talk about work—she's the co-owner of the bar—and on rare occasions we have sex, which to be honest is probably more satisfying than when we lived together.

My mother has no idea that all I've wanted these past few years is to get a divorce. I can't even broach the subject with her. The bottom line with her is what the church says, what the bible says, what God says.

So I keep living the way I'm living, hoping for the best, but I know that eventually something's going to have to give. So

I live my life to the fullest until it does. I love my club, I love Toronto, I love the women in this city, I love my life. Until I get an STD, or overdose, until I get AIDS or get hit by a taxi running across Queen Street, I'll keep on living this way. At least I'll go out with a bang. I'll be able to say I really lived my life.

Nicki

Bathurst and Lawrence, where my dad's cousins live, is like an Orthodox Jewish paradise. All the houses look the same; four or five bedrooms, a basketball net and two fancy cars parked in each driveway. My cousins live on a street called Glengrove, which has an Orthodox synagogue half a block from where they live, and at least three others within walking distance.

It's such a bracha, *a blessing, to be immersed in the Jewish community here, you'll see Nili, you'll love it. We'll help you*, they promised. They really tried to. They were nice, and they were obviously sincere in their beliefs, but it was hard to connect with people who thanked God so often. At first it was interesting to people watch. Men with long beards, white knee socks, black suits, black wool coats, and huge brown fur hats roamed the streets. Their wives walked behind them, their skirts sweeping the ground, with five or six kids, little boys with short hair, and one curly corkscrew curl over each ear called *payot, kipot*, or skull caps clipped, tightly on, *tzitzit*, or white vests with tassels on them, coming out of their starched shirts. Little girls in long-sleeved cotton dresses, patent leather Mary Janes and white tights, skipping, laughing. They'd cross the street if they saw me coming, me, in my shorts and tank tops on *shabbat*.

It quickly became depressing. Aside from my cousins, who barely spoke to me as it was, I had no human contact. The wives would give me the slit eye as I passed, the husbands would stare at the sidewalk.

I'd wander around Bathurst Street when I got bored, but it was no better. It was full of kosher bakeries, kosher chocolate shops, kosher frozen yogurt places, kosher pizza parlours. There was even a place called Diamonds and Donuts, a store that was a kosher coffee place and a jeweller, a place where you could have a muffin or a smoothie, and buy a diamond necklace, if you were so inclined.

Among my other discoveries were four private Jewish schools, a kosher Chinese restaurant, and a Judaica store where the windows were full of games and stickers designed to make religion seem fun for kids.

My cousins were always trying to get me to bake challah bread with them, to go to synagogue on Friday nights or Saturdays, to go listen to some rabbi or some rabbi's wife speak about some holy subject. I tried to be respectful at first. These people had taken me in, and it was interesting to see a completely different world, but before long, I was suffocating.

When my uncle suggested he set me up on a *shidduch*—a blind date where the intended outcome is marriage—I panicked.

He's such a nice guy, he insisted. *He just graduated from a program for newly religious guys in Jerusalem.*

I shook my head. I knew what he meant. I had met people like that. They say, *Thank God*, or *God willing*, as often as other people breathe. They openly judge people's worth based on their level of religious observance. I couldn't take any more guilt about who I was. I figured out how to get out of the neighbourhood, how to take the subway from Glencairn Station.

I found downtown, and found my job at CDRR within a week. I stayed in a hostel until I met Lukas, and then moved in with him. I used my tips and extra money from my parents to take art classes. Eventually I figured out where I wanted to be.

My relatives haven't spoken to me since, but I bet they're praying for me, or sitting *shiva*, which is a week-long mourning practice that the Orthodox participate in when someone dies. I wish I was exaggerating but I'm not. I've failed them because I was exposed to their holy, restrictive lifestyle and I still choose to think for myself.

It makes me sad when I think of them, so I try not to.

Marlize

I didn't hear them when they broke through the back gate.

I didn't hear their heavy footsteps as they walked through the garden.

I didn't hear them fiddling with the window with the missing burglar bar.

I didn't hear the back window smash.

I didn't hear the footsteps in the house. I didn't hear my dad gasp for air, stagger to his feet, get tied up.

I didn't hear our dog yelp as they kicked and drugged him.

I didn't hear my dad as he told them where the safe was, where the keys were. I didn't hear my dad say, no, no one else was home.

I didn't see the look of terror on his face when they found me, but I saw their faces, the mix of joy and greed, like children finding a pile of sweets they didn't know was there. There were three guys, and one of them wore an Adidas jacket, purple with silver stripes. He was the leader. I tried to forget what they all looked like.

I tried to forget the deep scar above Purple Jacket's lips, and the shakily drawn number twenty-six tattooed on the right side of his neck.

I could never forget how fearless he was. He looked me right in the eye, like he belonged in my house, and I didn't. He smiled at me when he held the knife to my ribs.

I could see the gun in his pocket.

I was in my room. I had a white canopy bed, a dresser and a cupboard full of dance leotards, tutus, pink ballet shoes, and school uniforms. I had a small desk in the corner, with a laptop and some speakers.

I had a Fokofpolisiekar poster taped to my door. They were an Afrikaans punk band, guys from not far from where I lived, in Belleville or Parow, who'd somehow become really big. Their name meant Fuck Off Police Car, and when journalists wrote about them in Afrikaans newspapers, they'd leave out the swear word; even in a headline, they'd write *polisiekar*.

My friends and I would laugh about it, how conservative adults were.

It was the beginning of December, summer. I was three weeks away from finishing high school, and two months from dance company auditions.

I'd been listening to music, chatting to my friend Lanelle on MSN messenger. We'd been talking about Obzfest, a music festival coming up. She was telling me about Riaan, a guy she liked, asking me what I thought if we all went together. A Chris Chameleon song was playing.

Purple Jacket grabbed my arms and tied them behind my back. I felt his knee jab me in the stomach and then I realized I was on the floor. He was on top of me, pinning me to my carpet. He spread my thighs apart and I felt his left knee pressed against my crotch. I was wearing shorts and a t-shirt.

He said, *You're pretty.* He was inches away from my face.

Do you have a boyfriend? I shook my head. *You want a boyfriend?* He put his hand on my chest, near my collarbone. I swerved, shook, tried to do everything I could to move away from him.

He punched me in the face. *You're stupid.*

How old are you? I shook my head. I wouldn't talk. I wouldn't make a sound.

He grabbed my breasts, tore my t-shirt. He unzipped my shorts.

You ever have sex before?

I kicked him, used all the dancer strength in my thighs, kicked him in his side. I felt one of his ribs crack.

He screamed. It was loud, shrill. The other two guys came running in. Purple Jacket smashed me in the stomach with his fist. He lifted me like I was as light as a piece of paper. He cut my shorts off. He took his knife out and stabbed me in the thigh, above my knee. I was bleeding. I didn't know it but the blade had sliced a nerve. I stopped moving.

The two guys watched as he entered me. They were waiting for their turn.

My mind left my body. I closed my eyes. I was onstage,

dancing the lead in *Swan Lake*.

When all three of them were finished, they picked me up and tied me to my chair.

The ropes were biting into my arms, thighs and ankles.

My mom and my sister were out. It was early, around 7:00 in the evening. I knew because at some point I could hear the faint voices of Derek Watts and Bongani Bingwa—hosts of a current affairs show that my dad loved—floating in from the living room.

My dad had a ritual every Sunday night. He would watch TV, starting with the news show, sitting on the couch, drinking beer, or brandy, or *witblits*, Cape Town moonshine. He worked for Telkom, the phone and internet company, doing marketing. He worked Saturdays, so Sunday was the start of his weekend. He'd drink and smoke Marlboros, with our dog, Tex, a brown Labrador mix lying at his feet. Sometimes he'd have friends over but that night he was alone. Like most South African homes, our house was one-storey, and open plan. From certain angles in our respective rooms we could actually see each other.

I didn't hear my mom open the security gate.

I didn't hear her car pull into the driveway.

I didn't hear her or my sister walk up the stairs to the kitchen door, or unlock the three separate locks and one gate to get inside.

I didn't see the looks on their faces when they found out what was happening.

I didn't see my mother or my sister before they were attacked, and I didn't watch them get shot.

I didn't see them struggle or try to fight back. I didn't see the life drain out of either of them, didn't hear the last things they said, or tried to say before they died.

I don't know if my dad tried to defend himself, if they overpowered him. Out of the corner of my eye, I watched the big guy in the red shirt drag him over to my room, still tied to the white wooden chair from the living room. Red Shirt and Black Shirt wanted to have a turn with me. I saw my dad cry as they both forced themselves inside me. I was bleeding, dripping onto the floor. I stopped fighting. I closed my eyes and heard my dad scream. I heard him beg for them to kill him. I heard the guys laugh.

I don't remember hearing the security company coming. I don't know when my dad pressed the panic button, and why it took them so long to get there. I don't know when the police came.

I remember feeling nothing when they all finally arrived.

I don't remember the questions they asked us. I don't remember the funerals.

I live every day with the guilt of outliving my sister and my mother. I know it's unfair, and I can't figure out the reason.

It doesn't seem right that life went on. It doesn't seem right that it had to.

Lukas

I lose my temper with her today 'cause I'm pissed as fuck to begin with.

It has nothin' to do with her, and we both know it.

A stupid conversation I overheard today at work sets me off into a world of flashbacks. It doesn't help that she stands there when I get home with her big cow eyes that always look bulgy and soft and kinda dumb lookin'.

Cows look at everyone, even the meat slaughter guy, with an incredible, stupid amount of love. You give them grass and a small pen and food, just basic shit and they'll do anything for you. It makes me sick sometimes, how Nicki acts. She'll literally do anything I ask her to do because I've given her a place to live, I cook her food and sometimes I tell her I love her.

I mean, it's fucked up.

She doesn't know shit about me, but she thinks she does and that's what scares me most. She's always reading into every little thing I do, tellin' me who I am, and what I'll do.

So I get mad. I go out for a bit. Kick the door in on my way out. Break her stupid ceramic vase that's in my way. Go and pound the shit out of a punching bag at the gym. Go for a run. Call my buddy and go out with him. Go back to his house, watch *The 40-Year-Old Virgin*. Crash on his couch.

In the morning, when I go home, she's the one apologizing, cryin', sayin' she was worried about me, do I know what I mean to her, all that pathetic shit, and I just can't deal with it. Guilt's eating at me—chewing on my muscles, and the marrow in my bones, threatening to do me in, right then and there.

Nicki's cryin', eyeliner smudged, black tears comin' down her cheeks.

I give her a hug. I say, *I love you, I gotta go to work,* and I go without tellin' her anything.

No one ever tells you how it's supposed to be, how these things are supposed to work, how much to share, and what to do if the person refuses to love you anymore once they know what you're hiding.

I sometimes think I might love her, and I'm back at work, mopping blood off hospital floors, listenin' to some dumb shit fifteen-year-old brag how he just has a fractured leg, but the dude he beat up is in ICU.

I have to try not to explode at him today. I have to try to keep it in check. I have to control every urge to tell this stupid kid that the *Youth Criminal Justice Act* isn't going to protect him from shit.

I have to control the urge to tell him that he's probably ruined his life.

Take it from me, kid.

Marlize

My sister Claudette started using my dad's old Minolta single lens reflex camera when she was five. He'd take her for walks near where we lived on a Saturdays, and she'd take pictures of flowers, of trees, of people passing by. My father glowed at this little girl who could master such a serious instrument without seeming to be intimidated by it. As she got older, he'd buy her *National Geographic* magazines and art books. He enrolled her in painting classes, in sculpting and life drawing. Claudette always wanted to try everything.

She started making short films in her last year of high school and won bursaries to two universities. In her first year she dressed like a hippie, wearing loose clothes and putting beads in her hair. She always smelled like sandalwood oil mixed with *dagga*, or weed. She actually looked and even smelled a lot like Nicki, which is part of why I find Nicki so irritating.

Claudette's boyfriend Tshepo was Setswana. He'd grown up in Soweto but had always gone to private schools so he spoke without a trace of an accent. He wanted to be a filmmaker, too. They talked about starting a company that made documentaries when they graduated. He called her Monet, because the painter's first name was Claude, which is what a lot of her friends called her. He told my sister that her eyes looked like aquamarine water lilies. When they first started dating, he wrote her a letter that said that she was so beautiful she could've been one of Monet's subjects. *You inspire great art*, he told her.

My mom always treated Claudette with a combination of admiration and fear, like she couldn't quite work out who she was or where she came from.

My mother worked part time as a teller at a First National Bank not far from where we lived. She sometimes went to church on Sundays which annoyed my father to no end. She considered herself spiritual, loved yoga, meditation, homeopathic medicine, astrology and other new age stuff my father dismissed as crap.

It's all a waste of money, he used to yell at her.

It makes me happy, she used to tell him quietly.

I think Claudette was a sign that my father's life was on track—that he could be who he wanted to be and have the kind of family and legacy he wanted to have despite where he came from.

At the funeral, paid for by my grandparents, and held in their church, we ignored the speeches, trapped in our own thoughts. I think I cried, a little. My grandparents cried but my dad was stoic.

After the guests cleared out, he threw himself on Claudette's coffin, bawling, smashing the expensive oak with his fists.

It's not fair, he told the *dominee*, the priest who tried to hold him back. *Her life was stolen from us.*

She's in heaven now, the priest told him, smiling, *where no one can hurt her. She's with God now, doing God's work, along with your wife, smiling down on you and Marlize as we speak.* He put his arm on my dad's shoulder and my dad bristled at his touch.

Family and friends phoned us, asked how we were feeling. If I'd been honest, I would've told them that I wasn't feeling much of anything. My dad and I were supposed to lean on each other in our time of need. We didn't talk about the rape because it was too horrifying. I had nothing to say about it and neither did he.

We couldn't say a single comforting word to each other. Any way of justifying it would have been a lie. We didn't give each other false hope. We both went to bed the night after the service, our rooms a passageway apart, the scenes of the crimes. We both cried until our bodies gave in and passed out. The next morning we tried to talk over breakfast, but no small talk came, and the heavy talk was too heavy for 7:00 a.m. We decided to avoid each other as much as possible. We moved in with my mom's parents the next week.

But we still found that we had nothing to say to each other.

Lukas

Waterville is this tiny town with a population of about 800 people. It's right next to Kentville, about fifteen clicks away or something. It's a quick zip off Highway 101, Exit 14.

The night I was driven in seemed to go on for hours. I dug my feet into the car mat, closed my eyes, tried to drown out my thoughts by focusing on the radio. One of those redneck country songs was playin', you know, the *she broke my heart, so I broke her jaw* types that you can't actually believe is real.

It hit me for the first time sittin' in the back of the van. There was no escaping it: I'd become my biggest fear. My whole life, whenever I misbehaved, I was told that if I didn't straighten up, I'd end up in Waterville. It was like when your dad threatened you that your spending would land the family in the poorhouse, or when your mom said your shenanigans would send her right to the loony bin.

I couldn't believe it had actually happened.

I was freaked out by how ordinary the town looked. Waterville had a small airport, a Michelin tire factory where a couple of my friends' dads worked, a skydiving school that impressed the occasional tourist, a nursing home and the provincial youth detention facility on County Home Road.

They were gonna force me to live there, in secure custody for two years. Everyone there called it the youth centre, as if it was a giant rec room that kids could go to after school to practise their cheers for a fuckin' pep rally.

How about just calling it what it is, I thought, *a jail for young fuck-ups*.

There was one main street in the town that split off into two lanes. It was lined with pizzerias and tanning salons, a high school and a bakery. The detention centre looked depressingly normal, a beige low-rise with white walls, minimal furniture,

a receptionist like any office you'd walk into. I was wearin'
handcuffs when I walked in, but no one stared.

A youth worker named Jane showed me around like it was
some hotel and I was on vacation. She even said, *So you're going
to be here for a while, are you? Did it take you long to get here?*

I tried to keep my mouth shut so I wouldn't say something
stupid. I think I grunted. I fuckin' hated small talk. She gave
me a tour of the common rooms: a cafeteria, a gym, a pool, a
chapel and a nursing station. She showed me where the anger
management and substance abuse classes were held, told me
I'd be forced to participate daily. She showed me the cottage
where I'd be livin' and studyin', said something about finishing
some school credits, maybe gettin' my GED. I nodded. I'd have
my own bedroom but have to share a livin' room with a bunch
of strangers. Mine was an anger management cell.

The youth worker said she probably wasn't supposed to tell
me, but remember that seventeen-year-old dude from Digby
who was in the paper three weeks ago, for killin' his dad? His
name was Tom and his bedroom was next door to mine. On
the other side were these three girls from North Dartmouth.
One of them stabbed someone over in Halifax, just a stranger
sittin' next to her at a table in the Commons. She talked
about another guy, Winston, who stole a jeep, drove it high,
and killed some old lady. She said it matter-of-factly, almost
smilin', like this was just regular life for her.

There were six of us who shared the cottage. She was
surprised that I didn't have any priors.

You got me all wrong, I wanted to tell her. *I'm not like that.
I was protecting my girlfriend from a psycho. It was an accident.*
I knew she wouldn't believe me so I kept my mouth shut. We
were all the same to her, all potential psychopaths.

Bedtime, she said, *is at 10:30.* It was 10:05. *Lights out at
11:00*, she said. She gave me my schedule for the next day.
Wake up time was 7:15. *There's time for everything*, she said,
rest, food, studying, support, even a little socializing. She gave me
a blank notebook and a pen, told me to journal every night
before I went to bed. *You need structure*, she said, when I glared

at her. Jane obviously had no idea how I'd been raised. All I could think about was escaping.

I met Mylene, one of the Dartmouth girls, that night before lights out. She checked me out, and I smiled for the first time. She had almond-shaped eyes that had a hardness about them, but something about the way they glinted and stared me down made me feel like it was an act. A hip hop girl who was frontin', the girl next door with a nice ass. I could even see it through her baggy pants. I couldn't stop smilin' at her. She must have known I was checkin' her out, 'cause she walked right over. She told me about a stabbing that she and her friends had committed to land her there, this impish grin cracking those lips, and there was something adorable about how hard-core she was tryin' to seem. She hadn't killed anyone, or hurt anyone too badly. It was the adrenaline, she said, the rush of drawing blood. She told me she was a repeat offender, that this was her third time back.

I like it here, she said softly. *I got my own bed, the food is good, I got friends.* Her mother was a drug dealer, and she hadn't ever known her dad. She'd hated school, being dyslexic and an underachiever. Her teachers told her she had an attitude.

I told her I liked her attitude, and wanted to run away from this place and take her with me, throw her over my shoulder and carry her off somewhere. She laughed then stopped when she realized I was serious.

You can't run away from here, idiot. If you try, they call it breaching. They'll catch you and place you on ISS—Intensive Supervision and Support. Forget about ever getting any privileges, man. ISS is the shits.

I nodded, asked if she could introduce me to the other girls, Kelsey and Jay-Lee.

Kelsey had pimples all over her face and one of those skinny bodies that hadn't filled out yet. She was sixteen but looked about twelve. She had a homemade tattoo of a rose on her neck. Jay-Lee was tall and lean like a model, a caramel goddess who refused to look me in the eye. She told me that she got arrested this time for soliciting. The girls had known each other for years. Mylene and Jay-Lee were even from the same housing project.

They promised to help me fit in, to show me the ropes, and I was grateful. They helped me set up my room, and organize my shit. The next day, after class and anger management I found that they'd helped themselves to whatever money I'd had left in my wallet. I figured it was just the price you pay for gettin' in with the right people.

Mylene and I got together right away. She made the first move. We weren't allowed, so we kept it on the down-low, snuck around after lights out. Condoms were hard to come by sometimes but I managed to pull out in time. All those months, never got her pregnant once. She was into some weird shit—one time she burned the inside of my thigh with a lighter while she went down on me. Another time she cut me with a metal nail file right before I was about to come. She gave me three new scars. It was always exciting with her, always unpredictable. Mylene was definitely the best part of havin' to be in juvie.

Nicki

When I was in the army, I liked this guy, Amit. He carried some bags for me from our base on a day off, and we started talking. We clicked just when I didn't expect to meet anyone. He loved *The Simpsons* and wanted to go to university right when he was done with his service, instead of going to India and getting high like most of the guys I knew. He read feminist textbooks for fun. He was really into Betty Friedan, and kept trying to convince me to read her books. We were actually from the same town. He'd dated one of my friends when we were in grade eleven. I remember him always talking about bands I'd never heard of. He made me feel more intelligent, just being associated with him.

He wasn't my type physically. He had huge muscles, arms that belonged on a bouncer at a club. He scooped me up and lifted me off the ground on our first date and I squealed. He took charge of almost every situation. He taught me about smoking weed, and making a good drink. He loved that I'd gone to a girl's-only school. The first time we got drunk together in his mom's living room, I remember laughing, trying not to scream as he kissed my neck.

The neighbours, he kept saying, *the neighbours can hear us*, the ceiling spinning above our heads.

Ze sof haderech, I yelled, Israeli slang that means the end of the road, but for some reason, is what we say when things are really good.

I felt amazing. I lost my virginity to him that night, which I could barely remember after.

The next morning, he held my hair back as I vomited into his toilet, smoothed my face with the back of his hand, gave me aspirin and glass after glass of cold water.

He wanted to be a photographer, and he taught me how to take my first shots. He took black and white photos of me whenever we had private moments. He told me I looked like an American pin-up model. He made me feel like a goddess.

He dumped me for another girl after we finished our service, which made sense to me then, because deep down I'd never felt good enough to be with him. He'd always resented how good I was with people, was always angry when I got along with strangers and somehow stole the spotlight from him.

I haven't thought about Amit in a long time, but I get an email from him today telling me he's getting married.

Rak ratziti lehagid lakh, he writes, *I just wanted to tell you.*

It feels like a punch to the gut, like those Jean-Michel Basquiat paintings he showed me with the words *Sucker Punch* on them. I don't know why it bothers me at all, it's been so long.

I wanted to invite you, he writes, *if you're in Israel. The wedding is in two months.*

I delete the email without replying.

I decide to tell Lukas about it, because he puts his arm around me, says, *I can tell when something's eating you, girlie.*

I have no idea what that means, so I ask him.

You're looking some depressed is what that means.

I tell him about the email.

Why'd you delete it, he asks me. *Why didn't you say something?*

I shrug. *Like what should I say?*

Oh I don't know. Like you have a boyfriend, and you live in Canada, so you can't go? says Lukas.

I think about it for a second. *I really don't have what to say to him. To tell you the truth, I don't care if he's happy. Why should I care when he's getting married? It's just irrelevant information.*

He nods and pulls away, tells me how his ex-girlfriend who lives in Montreal is having some other guy's baby. He has this faraway look on his face that I can't read. It's clear that he cares that he isn't in her life anymore, but he won't tell me anything more about her.

He disappears after that, saying he needs to go for a walk. I have no idea what to do with myself when he does that. I struggle to figure out how to make the time pass. The one thing I wish I remembered about what Amit taught me all those years ago, was how to make a good cocktail. If we had more alcohol around here, I'd be all joy and giddiness.

I wish there was some upside to the fact that Lukas has a whole life that he doesn't want to share with me.

Lukas

When I first came to Toronto, I met this girl, Emily. She was from Aurora, and had just moved downtown. We were both afraid of seeming like outsiders, like we were bein' taken advantage of. She seemed like a girl I could've met back home. She once said she used to be terrified of the city, because she knew that good people got swallowed whole. She studied graphic design but had never actually lived downtown. She was twenty-two, and tiny, with short brown hair that flipped down over her ears, huge, wide eyes, and a trusting smile. Her laugh was like a five-year-old's—so loud it bounced off the fuckin' walls. Sometimes she'd snort when she laughed really hard, and then she'd blush and stare at the floor.

We met in line at a 7-11 on Queen just west of Bathurst. I was buying a bottle of water and a pack of smokes, Du Maurier, I think. Emily had a large slushie in one hand, and a huge bag of candy in the other—the squishy colourful kind, shaped like fried eggs, little Coke bottles and green and white frogs. She just started talkin' to me when I made eye contact. She said she liked mixing all the flavours together to make her slushie—Cherry Coke, grape soda, Mountain Dew—and even though it looked gross, it tasted like fireworks made of sugar were exploding in her mouth. She grabbed an extra straw, one of those thick red ones, and told me to try it.

Doesn't it taste like a kid's birthday party, she said, *like something you could've had when you were eight?*

It is good, I said, and then asked her to make me one too. I paid for both of them, and then I went home with her. *I got nowheres else to go*, I told her, and she nodded.

It's cool, she said, and I practically moved in.

We dated for about eight months. She had a vintage Nintendo, the kind from the early '90s, with the original Mario and Zelda games. I always wanted one as a kid. She read Archie comics and *Seventeen* magazine for fun. She was lookin' for a job, but her parents had given her some money to live and pay rent with for the first few months.

Emily reminded me of when I was happy, and free, when I was too young to know how fucked up everything was.

We talked a lot about our childhoods, what it was like to be little kids. I told her how much I'd loved playin' hockey— on the ice and in the street. She told me about her My Little Pony collection. Her favourite pony was a hot pink one with a highlighter-yellow mane, and a pair of sunglasses painted on her butt. The pony's name was Shady, and I always called her Shades after that when I was bein' affectionate. I even found this store in Yorkville that carried '80s' memorabilia and bought her a pony still in its original packaging. She told me she loved me that day and I thought she meant it.

We'd sit in her apartment, on her couch or her red beanbag chair smoking a bowl of hash or doing a little E and watchin' '80s' movies like *Fast Times at Ridgemont High, Weird Science* or *The Breakfast Club.* Her favourite was *Sixteen Candles.* Sometimes we'd watch cartoons she had on DVD, like *Scooby-Doo* or *The Smurfs.*

She got a job at a design firm on King Street not too long after that. She had to design logos for different companies. At first she was excited but then she got bored.

They want me to change the background from indigo to turquoise, she'd complain.

I'd just gotten my job at the hospital and we were workin' opposite shifts. She started goin' out with friends she'd made at work, goin' for sushi at King and Bathurst and to expensive lounges and clubs in Liberty Village.

I'd tell Emily my dream of movin' back to the country somewheres, and she'd roll her eyes at me.

She got her hair cut shorter with chunky cherry-red highlights.

My boss says it's edgier, she said.

She got a nose stud in her left nostril, and a red, black and blue tattoo of a geisha on her right arm. She said it meant something to her, but I wasn't listenin'. I wouldn't go with her when she got it because I don't like tattoos on girls. She didn't care what I thought so I figured I didn't need to be there.

Even her clothes started to change some. When she went out, she wore shorter skirts and see-through lace tops with black bras underneath. She started wearin' tons of makeup, even buying thong underwear and gettin' bikini waxes. She was tryin' to be sexy, but she'd looked much prettier to me before.

I liked you all natural, down there and everywhere, I told her but she started cryin'. *I loved how you looked the night I met you.*

I'm trying to be more of a woman now, she said. *I'm doing this for both of us.*

Emily kept sayin' she loved me, but I didn't believe her. I wasn't even sure if I loved her anymore. I told her the truth one night.

I'd finished my shift at 2:00 a.m., and she was stumbling in from a club. She was drunk, talkin' louder than normal, laughin' hysterically at nothin'. She smelled like cigarettes and sweat and cheap cologne. I told her about the fight, about my ex and my kid and bein' in juvie. She yelled and cried and kicked me in the shins before throwin' me out. She said she was blocking my number from her cell phone and havin' her locks changed because she'd given me her spare key.

But Shades, it's me, I told her. *You know me. I get you. I get all the things you like, the movies and the games, the way you're like a kid. I love that about you. There's no other guy in the world who'll get you like I do. Don't you think what we have is some special?*

Her face crumpled while she thought about it, but she pushed me outta the door.

She never talked to me again, and crossed the street to avoid me when I ran into her this one time, on Strachan. She looked drunk, kind of stumbling, but still sexy. I had this feeling I'd fucked up, that I'd lost something good I'd never be able to get back. I felt sadder in that moment than when she broke up with me. It really hit me that I'd never see her again.

I know I could never tell Nicki the truth about me either. I know that no matter what, I don't want to risk losin' her too.

Marlize

I was angry all the time. Grief bored itself like a worm into the ventricles of my heart, squeezing out rage and tears without so much as a trigger.

I wanted to *klap* people: the waitresses at the cafés near our house, the corner shop owners, the bartenders, the acquaintances that called to give their condolences.

They asked stupid questions, like how I was feeling, saying what a terrible tragedy it was, as if I didn't realize it myself. I'd nod, rub my fingernails against the corners of my eyelids to keep the tears in, but all the time I was shaking with fury.

How did they think I felt? *Fucking idiots*, I kept thinking. Nothing anyone said could make me feel better for more than a minute or an hour at best. I'd have to live with it for the rest of my life, the violation, the loss, and the searing daily pain of being alive.

My father took me to a therapist in Vredehoek, in the Cape Town city centre, near the City Bowl. The name meant corner of peace and my dad, who hadn't previously believed in anything, took it as a sign.

The psychologist, Alet Viljoen, agreed to see us at her home office when she heard the story. She was pretty with dark hair and fine-boned wrists. When she looked at me her gaze was penetrating but not appraising. We sat in a light-filled room that overlooked the street. I sat on a white leather couch, my dad on a wooden chair. Alet sat on a pile of pillows on the floor, at her own insistence. The room was lined with bookshelves filled with English and Afrikaans books. There was a small piano in the corner.

My ex-husband played, she explained when she noticed me looking. The view of the city unfolding below us was spectacular. The mountains seemed close enough to touch.

She prodded me to talk about what happened.

I'm not comfortable talking about my attack in front of my father, I said, the words falling cold and hard from my mouth like marbles.

I fucking witnessed it, man, he yelled, but I ignored him. I didn't want to talk. I listened to him instead.

My dad talked about how beautiful Claudette was, how well she did at everything she'd ever done. She'd had so much promise.

He didn't talk about my mom, how they met, or what she'd meant to him, or even that her death was sad. He cried about my sister, how captivating she'd been as a baby. How strangers would stare at her tightly coiled ringlets and ocean eyes and tell my parents how beautiful she was. How she skipped a year of school. How early she had started to read. How many people had loved her. My dad was spluttering and sniffing and Alet was passing him the tissues and telling him how much she admired his sensitivity, how it was so healthy that he was expressing his emotions.

I went to visit her by myself the next week and I told her about the attack. I tried to tell her just what she needed to hear and no more.

It wasn't my first time, I lied to her when she asked. I wanted her to think I was normal. *His name was Jaco, and we're not together anymore. We haven't really talked since the funeral. I've been avoiding his calls.*

I told Alet that Jaco was the brother of a friend of mine, a friend whom I used to dance with. I met him after a rehearsal one day. He checked me out from across the room, and yelled *nice legs* at me.

For some reason, I heard *nice pants*, and said, *Thanks, they're my sister's.* He laughed and asked for my number. We dated for nearly a year after that. He was twenty and from Belleville. He had velvet eyes and hair he bleached blond and wore in little spikes. He was a musician, and worked at Musica, a store in the local shopping centre. His touch was gentle but since the rape I couldn't stand to feel his hands on me anymore. I didn't want his gentle words. I wasn't who I had been and I never could be again. I couldn't sit around listening to music, joking and kissing.

My sister had never trusted him. *You* doffie, she snapped at me one day. *He's cheating on you with a friend of Anika's.* I didn't want any more reminders of how much everything I'd once had no longer existed.

Alet mentioned something about a change of scenery, of exploring my options overseas. She told me that my dad said that he and my grandparents were willing to pay for it, and help me to organize the paperwork.

Your father is a great man, she told me on my way out that day. *He loves you and is willing to do anything to help you through this.* I shrugged.

I never saw Alet Viljoen again, but I know that my father kept seeing her for months after I left. I know that she helped him to feel less guilty about my mother, about my sister's death and what happened to me.

I hope she helped him to feel that there was nothing that he could've done to protect me or save them.

I think that she's helped him to move on. And I don't know how I feel about that.

Lukas

Kentville is kinda like that movie *Pleasantville*: manicured and so litter-free it wins awards. It's full of one-way streets (you can always spot a visitor because guaranteed, they'll drive up or down the wrong way), one school, King's County Academy, that goes up to grade eight, that has a Superstore next to it where all the kids go buy taters for lunch. I used to take a toonie and a quarter in my pocket every day in grade seven and eight to buy a medium-sized cardboard box of thick fries drowned in vinegar and ketchup. A couple of times I forgot my wallet, and rumours started with the kids that my parents were broke. The rumours reached my mom two hours later and she told my dad as soon as he got home that night. He chased me around the house with his belt for two hours.

I hated how tight all the adults were—how everyone knew my parents, and how much shit they talked about everyone. One time I left my coat at school one day in March, and the cashier at the Superstore, who was a friend of my aunt's, called my mom as soon as I left.

You want people to think we're poor, my mom yelled, *like we can't afford to get you a coat?* My town was all about appearances, lookin' all well-adjusted and happy.

I think my parents did okay, they had money, food and basic shit, but there was always this feeling of not havin' enough. My dad did his army shit, and my mom worked secretary temp jobs she hated, but her work would dry up for a while and my dad would yell at her, and she'd cry, but then they'd calm down and go right back to ignoring each other. Staying married no matter what was what they cared about.

My dad bought my mom flowers and chocolates on her birthday—red tulips and Turtles, same thing year after year—and jewellery, usually some kind of silver bracelet or necklace, on their anniversary. On those nights, she'd get all dressed up in a long black dress, her hair pinned up, makeup on, and they'd seem almost happy. The rest of the time she'd walk around in worn jeans and stained sweatshirts, hair hangin' around her face.

They hardly spoke, not even to argue. When I was young, around five, they'd scream at each other through the night, but by the time I was seven or eight, they stopped. She'd wash the dishes every night after dinner and leave her wedding band on, stare out the window when she was done, twirling her ring absently.

My dad would just say he forgot to put his on that morning.

He'd say, *I hate wearing jewellery; I don't wear a watch, or bracelets or necklaces either. You get that, don't you, Luke?*

I nodded. I told him I didn't like wearin' any jewellery either.

Good man, he'd tell me, shakin' my hand. *Don't you ever let some broad force you to wear a ring.* Sometimes if he was drunk, he'd make me promise. I'd say it but I didn't know why it mattered.

If my mom was havin' a good day she'd tell me what my dad was like when I was too young to remember. We'd go on family vacations to the South Shore, take road trips together and have picnics. She'd tell me about how they met at a high school football game, how my dad went right up to her and just made her laugh. She said my dad used to be fun; he'd take her on picnics and out to pubs. She said all the good memories made up for the bad times. I asked her why she stayed with him if he made her so unhappy.

Better the devil you know, Luke, she always said. *At least you always know what you're gonna get.*

When he died, she was single for about a year before she married my stepdad. I got to walk her down the aisle, while everyone cried and told her how much happier she'd be. My stepdad moved us to an army base in England when I was in grade nine. My mom assumed our financial troubles were over. He got promoted to Colonel with some big salary increase. My mom was broken-hearted about having to sell her house. He sweet-talked her and promised her all kinds of shit then cheated on her with a bunch of other military wives. My mom left him around the time I was in grade ten, when I was back home in the Valley. She stayed in England though, and met this geography teacher Phil. He was teaching at a school just a few blocks from the base, and he was from New Brunswick. A few months later they moved to Moncton.

I was glad that my mom wasn't around for my sentencing, that she didn't have to hang her head to avoid the glares and judgements of neighbours who woulda thought she fucked up by havin' me turn out like this. She knew I'd been sent to Waterville, she heard about it, but she stayed away. Maybe she couldn't handle it, maybe it was Phil's decision, but I didn't blame her.

If I'd finished my sentence we might be in touch right now, but I didn't. I had six months left and I couldn't fuckin' take it anymore. I'd been there almost two years and I was suffering, feeling isolated. Most people I was close to, including Mylene, had been released. I was sick of being a prisoner, havin' group circle, doing alcohol and drug rehab, talkin' about the stupid twelve steps and surrendering to a higher power I didn't believe in. I thought about escape for weeks. It was the middle of winter and they wouldn't let us keep our shoes in our rooms in case we decided to try and run.

I piled on every pair of socks I owned, all twelve of them, and ran shoeless into the snow. I jogged all the way back to Kentville, which took an hour. Maybe it was the adrenaline, the rush of doin' what I wanted to do instead of listenin' to commands, but I wasn't cold. I showed up right in the middle of the night at my buddy Mike's house, threw rocks at his bedroom window until he woke up and let me come in. The next morning at around 7:00 he drove me into Halifax. He loaned me some cash and I took a train straight to Montreal—no shower or nothin', he just gave me a pair of his shoes.

Maybe it was because I only had six months left, or maybe they just had bigger fish to fry, but I think the Waterville folks stopped searchin' for me after a while.

I know I can never go back home.

My ex-girlfriend Cheryl met me in Montreal with our kid. She'd been waitin' for me to get out. I think she felt sorry for me. The kid was almost two, and I hadn't seen him in so long, I cried. I tried to get her to move there, but she wouldn't. Her and James went back to the Valley and I kept going southwest, to Toronto.

I've been runnin' for so long I don't know what it's like to slow down. I never sleep through the night. I can't remember what it's like to talk to my family. I don't know what it's like bein' completely open with a girl. I've forgotten what it's like to live a life that's not drowning in guilt and lies.

Marlize

We're walking east on Queen toward his street, Brookfield. It's a Tuesday night in February, and it's completely deserted. We're the only people on the street for two blocks. Even the homeless people are inside somewhere. We pass expensive coffee shops and a Starbucks on the corner at Dovercourt.

Dez makes a face. *Is disgusting how they're commercializing our street, no?* I nod, slowly. *It makes me so mad*, he continues, *to see a unique, artistic place lose its personality. They're going to turn this whole street into an outdoor mall.*

I find his passion for the area oddly sexy. *I hadn't thought about it*, I admit.

Everything's going to get more expensive, rents and building leases are going to go up, musicians are going to move farther and farther west. He sighs.

We pass a snow-covered park and a wall with big white graffiti letters that say *You've Changed.* The only sounds are the gently grinding metal clicks of the occasional streetcar passing on the tracks.

It just worries me, he continues, *because all this wealth brings in a totally different crowd.*

I think about it. Ice and salt crunch under our shoes. *Wealth could work in our favour*, I say. *We could triple the prices of food and drinks and cover, and people would probably be happy to pay.* He grins.

I'm not wearing gloves and my hands are turning red. After a few blocks I grab his hand, and he surprises me by squeezing mine back and tucking it into his pocket. I feel my face break out into a smile, my cheeks cracking in the cold. It's a perfect moment.

His house is bigger than I expect, with red brick and pine trees outside. It has three floors. *I rent my basement out to friends*, he says. *They have a separate entrance, on the side.*

He gives me a quick mini tour of the main floor then takes me up to his bedroom. He takes off his coat and helps me out of mine, dumps them on the floor.

We sit down on the bed. His sheets are black.

There are books piled up beside his bed, business textbooks and Stephen King novels in Portuguese. He's taking a business course two mornings a week at George Brown College.

I like to highlight, he says, pointing to a pile of neon pink and yellow pens.

You're cute, I say, and he kisses me. *I had no idea; this is a whole different side of you. You're all serious and business-y.*

There's a lot you don't know about me, he says, and I can't tell if he's joking.

I like those Post-it note things, marking what pages I have to read in different colours, I say. *I should give you some.*

He laughs. *Who's the serious student now?*

I sigh. *I'm trying. It's hard, but I'm trying. I'm trying to get something out of it. It's just, I can't believe I'm here sometimes, you know? Here in Canada, at university, studying things I never wanted to study, not dancing. It's so frustrating—I hate my classes, they're huge, I never know what's going on, no one cares if I actually go or not. If I don't understand, I mean, you think I'm going to put my hand up in a class of three hundred people? Or if I disagree with a point, which by the way, I do all the time. My English literature professor is a doos, as we say in Afrikaans or as they say here, a douche.*

He laughs. *God, I hated school when I was younger. I couldn't wait to be done, to get out, to live life.* I nod. *I'm taking these courses because I have to now, but between you and me, Mar, I wish I didn't. I wish I were more—how do you say it—a natural? I get no pleasure in having to work so hard.* He gets up, walks over to his vinyl player, pulls out a Ramones album. I grin, close my eyes as the chords to "I Don't Want To Grow Up" start to play.

He sits down next to me on the edge of his bed and I pull him close, and kiss him. *You're perfect*, I tell him, as he starts unbuttoning my shirt.

He kisses my neck, unbuckles my belt, unzips my jeans, then stops.

I almost never bring girls here, he says. He looks nervous.

All I can hear in my head is *almost*. Almost isn't never. I try not to think about it.

I feel special, I say, try to kiss him again.

He flinches and starts to stand up. *I don't know if I'm ready for this,* he says. *I haven't had a girlfriend in years. Soon you'll want to come here all the time, be together all the time, all official, and I don't know if I want that. I see the way you look at me sometimes. I don't know if we want the same things, Marlize.*

I look at him. I'm tired of lying, to him and to myself.

I think I do want to see you every day, Dez. I really like talking to you, and being with you. I actually trust you. I think you might be the best person I've met here.

Why do you like me so much, he says, his voice getting louder. *I don't like it, I don't want you to, it adds this extra level of stress that I don't want, that I never wanted, to my life. I was trying to avoid all of this,* he says, gesturing wildly to himself, to me, in circles to the air around us.

I do up my jeans, get up to leave, grab my coat from the floor. *I like you,* and I pause for a second, try to organize my thoughts, try to get it out. *I like you because sometimes when we connect, when I say something weird or we're talking about something, we both know about it, and you understand me, I mean, really understand. It makes me feel less alone for a second.* I stare at my hands, at the thin curving lines in my palms. I say the next part quietly, not sure if he hears me. *It makes me feel like it's possible for me to be happy, does that make sense?*

I don't look up at him, just grab my bag, slip into my high-heeled boots and close the door behind me.

It's just this kind of understanding that he spends his life trying to avoid.

I understand now.

I'm crying as I walk down his driveway, nearly tripping on my heels, on the black ice.

I slide and try not to fall. When I get to my street, I reach into my coat pocket for my keys and realize they must have fallen out somewhere on his floor.

I don't want to, but my roommate's not home, so I call Dez.

He apologizes as soon as I say hello. *I just don't know what I want, if I'm ready for this*, he says. *I like you though. I really like you, and it scares me.*

He says he'll bring my keys in a few minutes, and I stand outside, shivering.

When he sees me, he puts his arms around me, says he's worried I'll get frostbite, and offers to come in and make me tea. I smile.

I show him how to make *rooibos*, South African tea, which I drink with milk and no sugar, and he says he'll have some too. He kisses me, tells me again that he likes me (and the tea), and that he's sorry. He asks me if I can give him one more chance.

I'll try, I say, because I want to understand him, and more than anything, I want to try to give him what he needs. It's strange to have no control of the situation. I wonder how long I'll be able to wait, realistically.

He falls asleep with his arm around me.

I watch him sleep, and stare out the window at the falling snow. It looks like liquid diamonds. It covers Queen Street and makes it look like the wilderness, untouched by civilization. It looks the same texture as beach sand. I finally fall asleep at around 7:00 a.m.

He wakes me up at 9:00, smoothing hair out of my eyes and stroking my cheek. *I really do have feelings for you, Marli*, he says. *Please be patient with me.*

I get up to walk him to the door.

Okay, I say, and sigh. *Okay. I'll do my best.*

He picks me up and carries me back to bed. *You really need to sleep*, he says. *I'll see you tonight, either at work, or if you're too tired, I'll come here after, okay?*

I smile. I sometimes fear sleeping because it leaves me completely defenceless.

I close my eyes and wait until he thinks I've fallen asleep. He kisses my shoulder and leaves my door open so I can watch him leave.

Bye, amor, he whispers so softly I think I've imagined it.

I really want to believe him.

Lukas

Our next-door neighbour is from Nova Scotia. I can hear it when she talks, the way she says *somewheres*, as in, *if you got somewheres else to be.* And the way she says *down home* about her hometown.

Where you from, I finally ask her this morning.

Bridgewater, she says, *you know, South Shore.*

No shit, I say. She nods. *My mom is crazy about the South Shore. She always wanted to get rich and have a cottage in Mahone Bay or in Chester. Beautiful down there.*

Yeah, she says, *it really is. Boring though.*

Yeah, I hear that, I say. *I'm from the Valley, from Kentville.*

Oh, I know Kentville, she says. *I love the Apple Blossom Festival.*

You sound like a tourist, I tease her. *What are you, a fan of the parade or something? I always hated that shit, it's so cheesy.*

She slaps my arm, but gently. *Yeah, but it's fun. The Valley's beautiful in the fall.*

Yeah, I guess so, I say. *Holy shit, you know, I think you're the first person I've met out here from home.*

She smiles. *You too.*

She has the longest eyelashes I've ever seen. She's curvy, with big blue eyes and blonde hair. She has big breasts and usually wears a tight shirt and jean shorts that look like cut-offs, all ripped and worn. She kind of looks like a sexy farmer's daughter or something, the kind of girl I never would've looked at twice growin' up, who suddenly seems so hot. I lean in towards her glossy lips.

I gotta go soon, she says. *My husband's picking me up.*

Husband? My voice actually squeaks a little as I say the word.

Yeah. I met him when I was livin' out west, in Calgary. He's from Ontario. I hate it here.

I laugh. A lot of people in Nova Scotia hate Toronto. People from Toronto who move there are always sayin' they're from Ontario. As if they're foolin' anyone.

I sigh. *Me too*, I find myself sayin'. *I really hate it here
sometimes.*

*Is the girl you live with, with the caftans and the Aladdin
pants, your wife?*

I shudder. *No, God, no*, I say, before I can stop myself.

She laughs. She touches the side of my face with fingers
that feel rough. *You'll meet the right person someday*, she says.

Yeah, I say to her, *thanks. Nice talkin' to you.*

When I think about it, I do care about Nicki. Sometimes
when I wake up sweating in the middle of the night, I just
wanna be able to wake her up and tell her why. I wanna hear
her tell me that it's okay. That she still loves me. That she
knows my past must have been a mistake. I wanna hear her say
that I'm a good person, that she can see I'm different now. I
want her to say she forgives me. I want her to help me forgive
myself.

Sometimes, when things are good, I fantasize about taking
her to see my hometown.

I actually miss it sometimes. I miss seein' all the apples in the
fall, the tiny flashes of red and yellow peeking through leaves. I
miss the glacial beauty at Christmas time, the frozen streams
that look like cracked opals. I miss the tiny red squirrels and
the tame little raccoons. In Toronto, the raccoons are huge and
in your fuckin' face. They look you in the eye and hiss when
they waddle past you at night, like gang members who know
they control the street.

I miss knowing where I'm goin' all the time without havin'
to even think about it.

What I like about Toronto mostly is Queen Street. I like
the way the stores just down the block from where I live are
open twenty-four hours. I like the way I can just grab a cab
off the street, no matter what time of night it is. I love eating
roti—those Caribbean wraps filled with meat, spicy chickpeas
with a side of rice and peas.

Nicki loves all the art galleries and the graffiti. She's
always talkin' about this mural near the train tracks behind the
Gladstone Hotel. She's always showing me photos of it—she

loves all the vibrant shit. Her favourite is this cowboy leaning against a bright pink background, with the words, *Laughter Solves Depression* in looping script.

I'm the opposite: I love the grime, the real-life feel of things, the mix of dollar stores and libraries, high school students and prostitutes, little kids and dealers. What I like most about my Parkdale neighbourhood is that I can disappear. No one knows me here. I can walk down my street or into the liquor store or onto the streetcar with no one hasslin' me, or thinkin' I'm bein' rude for not makin' eye contact or sayin' hi. I can do whatever I feel like doin' here—I can be whoever I want, and no one gives a flyin' fuck.

Dez

We got married in a Catholic church ceremony. The heat was sweltering, and when I stood close to her I could see beads of sweat forming above her lips and on her brow. The bridesmaids were sweating their foundation off, and looked like puffy blue clouds in their dresses. They looked ridiculous, so much hairspray and lipstick and fabric.

Adriana was beautiful, a princess walking down the aisle in a dress that showed no extra skin, just the outline of her amazing curves. She drove me crazy standing there, wanting to give herself to me, like a present to unwrap. I hadn't been able to see her until the ceremony; she arrived ten minutes late, according to our tradition here, and my jaw dropped. This woman wanted to be with me for life.

I really couldn't figure it out. She was older, twenty-six to my twenty-two. She had brown eyes that glistened when she was excited and flashed when she was angry. If I was talking like I was full of it, she'd call me *rei na barriga*, an arrogant king. I had to take her on like a million dates before she'd sleep with me. A million fancy dinners and walks on the beach. I'd never lived with anyone, but she had, and after a few months she said we should move in together. I was still living at home, anxious to get out of there, have my own life.

She had a good job in PR, made good money, worked hard. My dad had just died, and I was taking over his business, struggling to be an adult, pretending I had it together when I didn't. She gave me the stability I wanted but never had, and the chance to call myself an adult.

We got married after less than a year, talked about our goals of moving overseas, our ambitions, the money we both had. It just made sense. If we moved somewhere, like the US, we could have a business together; I could earn in dollars and send money home. I don't know if I knew what love was, but I wanted it. I knew my thing with Adriana was comfortable and in some ways, easy. I think she loved me, and I loved that for once I was doing what was expected of me.

We went to Disney World for our honeymoon. We were like two kids running around Florida, riding teacups and the "It's a Small World" rides, screaming on rollercoasters, eating hot dogs, kissing, holding hands.

It made us sure of where we wanted to go. When we realized we couldn't get into the US, Adriana suggested Canada. She was the one who did the research and found Toronto, with its huge Brazilian community and job prospects. She did the paperwork and got us in. It was her idea not to do just Brazilian food, to work it in somehow. I spotted the bar on Queen West, the dive with two pool tables, a tiny bar, some swivel stools. I was the one who did the work, checking out the scene, figuring out what was popular. It was my idea to embrace the sleaze. Calling it Casa de Rocha y Rolo was my idea. Hers was to shorten it to CDRR.

We made Brazilian food and drinks, but also served American junk food. We had five-dollar white trash specials, like mac 'n' cheese, and peanut butter and jelly sandwiches, along with rice and beans, the across-the-border special. It was the chef's idea, but it was brilliant. When we had the money we got a gambling license, put in mini poker tables and a slot machine. We built a small stage for local bands to play, got the kids who worked there to tell me who to hire, and what LPs we needed for the jukebox, fuck if I knew. We paid a graffiti artist to do the walls—hip hop-looking, rock 'n' roll, thick blacks and silvers. We tried to display local art.

Eventually we put in a theatre room upstairs, to play cool indie movies with no cover charge once a week. The university kids would come dressed up, corsets and boas for *Moulin Rouge*, army gear for *Full Metal Jacket*.

We had actually started making money when things started falling apart. Adriana was doing the books, doing the numbers, crunching and budgeting and figuring things out and I was doing every girl that came in. I couldn't help it. We hadn't had sex in months. All we ever talked about was business. We worked different hours, different kinds of work, we never saw each other.

One day she found me in the back room. I was fucking some girl, her panties around one ankle, my pants down, coming all over the girl's thigh, and Adriana waited til the girl slinked out, staring at the floor, then dug her nails into my face until it bled. She packed up her stuff and moved out that night.

This was more than a year ago, but still.

Adriana still owns half of the business, our apartment and a whole lot of other things. I probably could never have done anything without her. We don't talk that often, but she has power over me and she knows it.

It's hard for me to officially end it with her because I know I need her.

I don't love her, and I don't think she loves me.

I want to let go, have it officially be over, but I'm terrified. What if I'm nothing without her?

As far as Marlize, or any woman I've ever been with knows, I'm single. Completely and one hundred percent single, the full owner of my life, and this place.

Adriana has me by the throat, and could go for the jugular anytime just because she feels like it.

I probably don't deserve to be with either of them.

Marlize

The last conversation I ever had with my sister was a fight.

It started in person and ended over the phone and then by text.

It was on a Saturday, when she came over for lunch. We were having a *braai*—a BBQ outside.

My dad was cooking steaks dripping with blood and sauce, with *mielies*, or corn on the cob.

My mom had made a piece of fish, sole I think, and I was picking at it gingerly. She swore she hadn't used oil to flavour it but I tasted something, something more than just fish.

She shook her head at me, but said nothing.

Claudette sat down next to me, crunching food. She rubbed butter all over her *mielie* and I shuddered.

Eet, she kept saying, *fokken eet.* Eat, fucking eat.

I shook my head. *I am eating.*

She poked my ribs with a fleshy index finger. *You're too thin,* she said, *it's not healthy.*

Sies. Jy lyk vreeslik. Gross. You look terrible.

Jawellnofine, Claudette, I said, whatever. What a stupid way to try to convince anyone of something, by insulting them.

I ignored her for the rest of the day.

A parting shot before she left: *Men like women who look like women,* she said. *Not a bag of sticks.*

I ground my teeth. *Jaco seems to like me and my body just fine.*

She shook her head. *That's what you think,* she said. *Men are never satisfied with anything. You could at least try to take care of yourself. For you, not them.*

It was a weird thing for her to say, so unlike her, but I tried not to think about it. I remembered that she and Tshepo were having problems, possibly even about to break up. I tried my best to ignore her.

Later that night I went out with my friends. We played pool at Stones and bought some bottles of wine.

We piled into two cars and drove to Clifton Beach with some blankets. The band Boo! was playing as we drove. There were a couple of flame-jugglers tossing batons full of fire into the starless black sky.

Jaco pulled me onto his lap, poured me some kind of white wine. I was getting drunk quickly.

My sister called me and I had to get up, take a walk to get away from everyone. She said she'd seen my boyfriend out with a bunch of people, including attractive girls, that Friday night.

Kyk uit vir hom, she said, watch out for him. Maybe it was the wine, or the fact that I was actually out with friends, socializing, which was so rare for me, but I was really angry.

Why, I asked her, *can't you just let me be happy? Why must you judge everything I do?*

Because mom and dad don't give a shit, she said. *Someone needs to tell you.*

I hung up the phone on her.

She called back fifteen minutes later. *Nothing you do in your life is healthy*, she said. *You do everything to excess, you're always so obsessively focused—on dance, the boyfriend, your weight. Why can't you just be normal?*

But I love dancing, I said. I was crying. *It's my art form. It's my expression.*

Please, she said. *You're working yourself to death. You look like death. You're going to end up an anorexic with osteoporosis. You're going to die before you're thirty. I don't understand this obsessive focus of yours. I used to dance too, I was never like you.*

You were never as good as me, I said.

She was quiet.

All this work, she continued eventually, *all this reaching for something more, all this ambition is going to leave you disappointed.*

Dit's genoeg! I yelled at her. That's enough. *At least I have a direction. At least I know what I want from life and I have the confidence to go after it. At least I know what I'm good at it. At least I'm clear.*

Then she texted me to say that I should think about how to be a good person, a sister or friend, that I should forget the dance company and go to university, actually learn to create something of my own. *You don't even know what's happening in your own family,* she wrote. *You are so self-absorbed.*

I don't want to know what's going on with our parents & with you, I wrote back. *Did that ever occur to you? Need to focus. Major auditions in less than 2 mnths. Don't need any distractions.*

A final text from her, at 2:30 that morning.

Ek's jammer, Marlize. I'm sorry. *Want to understand how you feel.*

Ja, me too, I wrote back.

Laat ons later praat, she wrote. Let's talk later.

I didn't really want to.

I was afraid of not being able to take it, of crying as I vomited from my hangover into a sandpit that the boys built, knowing we wouldn't be able to hold our alcohol, Jaco smoothing my hair back, telling me that I'd be okay when I knew I wouldn't.

The last time I heard Claudette's voice was on Sunday night. I heard her and my mom walk in through the front door. I heard their keys and their shoes, my mother's heels clicking on the ceramic tiles near our door. I heard their voices. Claudette was talking so loudly.

They must have run into the robbers on their way out. To this day, I wonder what would have happened if they had come home ten or fifteen minutes later.

I was still tied up in my bedroom. I thought about screaming to warn them but I was too afraid to.

I wondered if they knew what was coming, the way people always seem to know in movies. What did they think about in their last moments?

Purple Jacket must have made a move towards my sister. I heard his voice, and my mother screamed, *No. No, stay away from her.* Maybe she threw herself on Claudette, or tried to push Claudette out the front door to protect her.

The next thing I heard was a gunshot followed by another. They were louder than I expected; a crack and then an explosion followed by dead silence.

The police told me later, when I pressed them, when I insisted that I had to know what happened, that the guy had shot them both in the face, that the bullets had gone straight through their brains.

I remember seeing their blood on the wall by the front door, thin lines dripping onto the white ceramic tiles. I vaguely remember the ambulance, the private security people, the police coming in. The paramedics kept saying BT, an acronym for ballistic trauma, which meant gunshot injuries. I caught the words *brain damage*, and *exsanguination*, which I knew meant bleeding to death. They pronounced my mother and sister dead on arrival at the hospital. One officer told us that crime and AIDS would kill us all one day. I remember him asking me detailed questions about what happened. I can't remember what I answered. My legs were so sore it was hard to stand.

I had to spend the next two nights in Valkenburg, the psychiatric hospital in Cape Town.

It used to be an asylum. A girl was screaming in the hallway, being restrained by two nurses as we walked past.

She's having a psychotic episode, one of the doctors told us matter-of-factly.

They swabbed fluids from my cheeks and my thighs and between my legs. They combed my body for hairs and fibres. They scraped under my nails. They filled vials with my blood. They gave me big, white pills that made me feel like I was floating. A part of me was terrified, and a part of me hoped they'd force me to stay.

They asked most about my sister. I had trouble remembering what happened to her. I kept asking how she was, and saying that I wanted to see her.

I kept forgetting that she was dead.

It took months for the facts to sink in. Even when they did, I wasn't sure I believed them.

Nicki

I have a part-time job aside from working at the bar. It's pretty sporadic, but the money's good.

I pose for a group of artists, some men, some women, at the art college where I study. I do it for the class on Thursday nights. All I have to do is take off my clothes and lie or stand in different positions for three to four hours while they draw me. It's easy and liberating. They don't see fat or cellulite, they see lines and contours and angles and shapes. I look at their drawings and barely recognize myself.

So this is what it's like, I think, *for people to see everything about you, but not judge you.* I feel like one of those naked three-year-olds running around on the beach, completely carefree, wanting to run off and build a sandcastle, knowing that no one is thinking anything's strange. It feels amazing.

I tell Marlize about it and she snorts. *It's good money*, I tell her, *and really fun. It's empowering.*

Why not do porn, she says, and rolls her eyes.

I think about what she said.

I flip through *Hustler* the next day at the convenience store across the street from work. I've looked at Lukas's internet porn. I think I could do either, if I had to. Sometimes people desperately need the money. But what I'm doing is about making art, and feeling fearless in my own skin. I wish Marlize understood the difference.

I like connecting with Lukas physically. I like how different he feels to any guy I'd been with in Israel. I've never been with a guy with a foreskin before. Even the guys I dated in the UK had been circumcised. I like the texture of Lukas's skin down there; I like the sensation of him inside me. I like knowing that I'm having an experience I never would've had if I'd stayed at home.

I tell him about what Marlize said to me, and he laughs. *She doesn't get you*, he says. *She doesn't get your art. You're so talented, Nicki. You're really gonna go places.*

When things are good, when he's being affectionate, he stares at me, and calls me his piece of art. He makes me feel like my body is a canvas that deserves to be displayed to the world. He makes me feel exotic and captivating.

I hope I do half as much for him as he does for me sometimes.

Marlize

Tshepo, my sister's boyfriend, came to visit me after the funeral. He said that according to his Setswana culture, he was in a period of mourning called *boswagadi*.

It means widowerhood, he told me.

In my culture, when your moratiwa, *your lover, dies, your whole family mourns with you. They shave your hair, and you eat special meat that's unsalted and unflavoured, called* mogoga. *In the olden days, in my grandfather's time, they believed that if your* moratiwa *died, you were impure, and dangerous to have around. You'd bring bad luck onto the village, onto the crops and cattle. Some believed that it was enough to stop the rain from falling. The death would have to be reported to the tribal authorities, who would bring a healer in, to cure him. He'd have to maintain proper distance from everyone around him and not get involved with another woman for at least a year. How do Afrikaans people mourn*, he asked me.

I shrugged. *We wear black clothes to the funeral, and in the time after that. If you go to church, there's this thing they do on New Year's Eve, where the pews are draped in black and purple, and they read the names out loud of people's family members who died that year, and have a kind of ceremony for them. My mom was religious. She made us go to it as kids. I think I was seven, maybe eight. Claudette was eleven or twelve.*

He nodded. *I loved your sister so much. She was such a unique spirit, so strong. I would've married her. I really consider myself a widower.*

I was surprised. *I thought you guys were arguing all the time*, I said. *What actually happened? She never told me.*

He shook his head. *We were fighting all the time. We decided to take a little break. We were nearly three years, you know. I was at this party in Woodstock, in someone's flat. We were smoking* dagga, *me and this Xhosa girl, Nompeliso. She was attractive, not beautiful like Claude, but attractive. We talked shit for a few hours. She wasn't brilliant like Claude, but she was bright, and funny. We had too much to drink, you know, it happens. It didn't mean anything. I decided to tell Claudette, because I loved her, and I thought she'd understand. She was furious with me. People make mistakes, I told her. Men are idiots. After our first year together, we took a break then too, and she was with that Afrikaans guy.*

I nodded. *Ja, our neighbour's son, Koos. I remember.*

I thought she'd understand, he said. *She was so upset with me. Ke a go rata, I told her, I still love you. She was my life, Marlize. We got back together, but she was still hurt. She never forgave me. I told her I didn't know if I'd been safe with Nompeliso, I couldn't remember. I'd been with Claude for so long, she was on the pill, I didn't buy condoms anymore.* He was crying now.

I got the results last week. I'm HIV positive, he said, and was silent.

When it finally sunk in, I asked him if he'd been with my sister after that night. He nodded. He'd gone out with her on the Friday night, two days before the attack. They'd slept together that night, the same way they always did.

He got up to let himself out, and apologized to me over and over. He even asked me to forgive him. I didn't say anything.

I was in shock, but it seemed futile to be angry with him. What difference did it make now, anyway?

Nicki

An explosion never sounds like you expect it to. It's like gunshots, they sound tinny in real life, almost fake. Explosions make the air quiver, make furniture and walls collapse, but for the first few minutes anyway, most people are too stunned to scream, much less to react. I've only witnessed one explosion, one *pigua* as we call it in Hebrew.

I was in a pizza restaurant, a Sbarro chain place in Jerusalem. It was one of my days off from the army, and some friends and I had decided to hitchhike to Jerusalem since none of us had a car. Since we were soldiers we could ride any bus in the country for free, as long as we had our uniforms, and our army ID. But we decided it would take us too long to get there, two buses from Tel Aviv, so many stops along the way. We decided *la'asot trampim*—to hitch a ride. A religious man with a white beard down to his waist picked us up and took us about halfway, to Lod.

A hippie guy and his girlfriend, who both had long hair and shell necklaces, shorts and Birkenstocks, took us the rest of the way. They had just gotten back from Thailand, and were telling us that when we were done with the army we had to go there. They told us about the beaches and the scenery, the great prices and the people.

Everything is "same same" there, the girl told us. *You go to one club or bar and someone in there tells you that you have to check out another one down the street. It's better, they tell you. "Same same, but different," whatever that means.*

I remember laughing at that. They loved it there, they told us. It was *chaval al hazman*, so intensely good that it was a waste of time even trying to describe it. They'd ridden elephants and bought amazing Le Sportsac knockoff bags that looked exactly the same, but had cost a fraction, and eaten mangos and sticky coconut rice with cashews every day. They'd gone there on their honeymoon. Their fingers glinted with braided matching gold wedding bands.

I remember thinking that I wanted to have what they had one day. I wanted to travel the world—Asia, Europe, Australia—with someone I loved.

We decided to go downtown, to King George Street. They dropped us on the corner of King George and Jaffa at around 1:30. We were starving, we'd all lost at least five kilos since basic training. We ordered our pizza to go—a slice each—I ordered one with tuna, corn and black olives, an Israeli special. It was hot so we all bought bottles of water or Diet Coke. There were four of us, myself, Meital, Liat and Tamar, in the same unit together. We had all sardined into the backseats, Tamar, who was tiny, sitting on Meital's lap as the couple drove. Liat and I were closest. Meital was bossy, one of those natural leaders that I found impossible to like. Still, I was happy we were all together.

We were leaving the place, crossing the street, when we noticed a guy in a fleece zip-up shirt, and a turquoise bandana, carrying a ripped guitar case. He was young-looking, maybe twenty or twenty-one. He had thick eyebrows and a moustache, a shaved head, and spindly legs. Our eyes met for a second, and he smiled. He had a glazed look in his eyes. We turned around and kept walking. He stood outside Sbarro. He must have been wearing a belt underneath his shirt, full of explosives, nuts, bolts and nails. He detonated his bomb on the patio, just before he passed the security guard.

The blast was louder than I expected. The store windows smashed and there was a full minute of silence before I heard children screaming. There was so much blood, people crouching underneath chairs turned upside down, lying on their backs and curled up in balls, afraid to move or unable to.

Liat and I crossed the street—we were in our army uniforms after all, and there were expectations of us—and we approached a little girl who was maybe two or three who was lying face-down in a pile of glass. Blood was streaming from her ears. Her body was warm, but when I reached down to turn her over she didn't move. Liat put her hand on my shoulder, and I realized I was shaking.

She's gone, Nili, she said to me, her voice trembling. The girl's mother walked over to us. She was howling, carrying the body of her five-year-old son. Her leg had been punctured by a nail, but she was alive. We stood next to her and cried until the ambulances started arriving.

Meital, who'd gone back for another bottle of water for the road, was killed instantly. Tamar, who'd run after her, was badly hurt. Fourteen others died and a hundred and thirty were injured.

Our commanding officer was furious with Liat and me for hitchhiking. *Don't you understand what could've happened? You could've all been killed. Do you have any idea how many terrorists pose as Israelis to pick up hitchhikers? And you didn't even take off your uniforms. You girls are idiots.*

Tamar was discharged shortly after, and we had a memorial service for Meital. Liat described her as a luminary who faced danger fearlessly. She talked about how her name, Meital, meant dewdrops, and that she would always think of her in the spring, in the early mornings when moisture gathered on the grass. I didn't feel anything for months—at first I was numb, and then I learned to compartmentalize it until I stopped thinking about it at all. It wasn't until I moved to Canada that I really thought about it—was settled enough to focus.

My people kill other people for the ownership of land in the name of religion and tradition.

Here's a secret I try not to tell anyone: I shot an Arab soldier the week after my basic training. We were passing through a checkpoint and the guy attacked me. I guess I looked the weakest, the least sure of myself. I'd just learned to fire a rifle so I only shot him in the arm. All that practice and my aim was still poor. It was self-defence, but still. It scared me how easily I could've justified killing a stranger.

Lukas

It's hard to describe the claustrophobia I feel livin' in a city where you can't see the skyline 'cause of all the big buildings, where there's so much noise you have to yell at the person you're with when you step out on the sidewalk. Where you can't see the stars at night, where every corner is packed with newspaper boxes and homeless people and crowds, where there's no open space.

Sometimes it gets to me, my chest gets tight and I feel some anxious. That's when I have to get outta my apartment, get outta downtown, walk over to the Greyhound station at Bay and Dundas, or the nearest GO station and hop on a bus or a train. I go wherever I can: Kitchener-Waterloo-Cambridge, Guelph, Pembroke, Oshawa, Mississauga, Oakville—small towns full of identical Lego houses, tiny patches of yard, a little grass and flowerbeds, and minivans parked out front. It's like a sweeter, bigger dream version of home. Pregnant moms runnin' behind little kids in overalls, setting up lemonade stands or drawing on the sidewalk with coloured chalk. Places full of chain restaurants like Jack Astor's and Montana's, Shoppers Drug Marts in strip plazas and overly air-conditioned malls.

I stare out the windows on the bus while it races through downtown, along Lakeshore. See the water glitter not too far away, feel the balloon in my chest deflate a little, see the bus pull onto the highway, the skyscrapers gettin' smaller with each block. I start to feel my breathing comin' back, stronger, closer to normal. When I see bigger patches of grass, taller trees in bigger clusters, fewer traffic lights, I breathe better. When I see hills, barns and fences, horses and cows, land going for acres, I start to feel like myself again. When I visit these towns, I walk around, talk to people that are more open to talkin' to strangers. I stop at pubs and have a pint or two of whatever they have on tap. Sometimes I make friends and occasionally I hook up with girls. It lets me get away from Nicki, from my job, and from myself. When I go to these places I can be any age from twenty-one to thirty-five. I can have any job and be from anywheres in Canada. I can be single or in a relationship, divorced or even widowed. I can even come home the next day and Nicki won't ask me too many questions. She wouldn't understand even if I explained it to her. Sometimes I need a vacation from myself.

My favourite town is called Aberfoyle in Puslinch, next to Guelph. It's a tiny place with an elementary school, and a classy restaurant where I eat the same thing every time: linguine with tiger shrimp. There's a bunch of tree-lined streets and a stretch of road with a few cars, an A&W Burger, a convenience store, a greasy spoon called Teesha's, a gas station, and a GO station. It reminds me so much of the Valley that when I first saw it I couldn't believe I was still in Ontario. Puslinch Lake isn't as pretty as the Atlantic Ocean and it doesn't have that strong, salty smell, but still, it feels kinda like gettin' an unexpected hug.

The people are warm and down-to-earth. You can shoot the shit with 'em, talk about the weather and nature.

I chat to a random guy in the convenience store about camping, and it brings back memories of camping trips to Middle Musquodoboit, when I was a little kid. I tell him about seein' my first moose—the way he stood there all majestic, seven feet tall, with these huge fuckin' antlers. I remember standin' there, shakin' at the sight of him, how my dad made me look away instead of starin' him in the eyes.

It's confrontational, he told me. We didn't have a camera that day, but I didn't need one. The moose's brown fur and knobby knees are permanently scanned in my brain.

The guy tells me about takin' his kids fishing, to a trout farm; he has a six-year-old and an eight-year-old, and I tell him about Tatamagouche, this little village where my dad took me fishing when I was maybe six. My mom would come with and pick blueberries, and we'd eat 'em for dessert. I remember the first time I caught a fish, a right tiny one that we couldn't even eat. I was so proud of myself, and my dad gave me this look like, *you're getting it, you're gonna be okay*, and I felt so good

I thought I was going to explode. It was this rare time where I felt totally loved.

The thing I miss most about Nova Scotia is the open spaces when you drive down the street. I miss Halifax, because even though I'm not a city person, as far as cities go, it's the perfect size. I like how every neighbourhood is different, how when you say the North End, or the West End, the Hydrostone, or the Commons, people know exactly what you mean.

I hate this bullshit of using intersections to describe Toronto. If you don't know the exact street, you don't know what the hell people are talkin' about. This place is huge and you never have that feeling like when a place belongs to just you and your own memories.

I remember there was a coffee shop on Brunswick I used to love, with the best breakfast specials, bagels, eggs, bacon, all that stuff—I loved goin' there just to think. I miss this Greek restaurant on Quinpool Road that I used to take girls to, and they'd think I was all cultured and shit. I miss all the pubs, where the atmosphere was so friendly and everyone sat for hours and drank and had a great time. I miss Pizza Corner, this intersection where there's three pizza places and a donair shop, the perfect thing when you're drunk at one or two in the morning.

I miss the layout of the city, the hills and winding roads that lead up to the Citadel and down to the harbour. I hate how flat Toronto is. I miss the way that water surrounds you almost everywhere you go, from the Bedford Basin to Point Pleasant Park to Bayer's Lake. I miss how easy it was for me to just talk to people and feel like we were clicking, naturally, instantly, on a bus, in a store, in a bar, even if we never talked to each other again. I miss that easy feeling where you can just talk shit to a stranger and they won't think you're a fuckin' freak. To be honest, I've forgotten how it feels.

Nicki

Alon was my first serious boyfriend.

When Lukas disappears for hours, when he stays out overnight and I don't know how to find him, I email Alon. I ask him about his life, how his new girlfriend is. He seems happy with her, so I never tell him how I really am. When things are good between me and Lukas, and I feel content, I don't talk about it either, because when you feel satisfied you just live in the moment, and hope it lasts. You never jinx it by talking about it.

Toronto sometimes still seems exotic to me with its cleanliness and its neurotic lack of overstepping anyone's boundaries. Sometimes I still can't believe how no one flips out about anything here. I've never seen people scream at bank tellers, or waiters or cab drivers chasing customers down the street demanding bigger tips. People also don't bond here with strangers over complaints about life, unless they're talking about the winter.

There's a feeling in Israel that life is harder than anywhere else, and there's an understanding people have that it's unreasonably hard to get by there. Here people go to university when they're so much younger, choose careers at the age of eighteen, or nineteen, and live a life that's so much simpler that they don't have patience for people who do anything else. Most of all, I can't get over the men here: unless they're drunk, they're afraid to touch or even talk to women. They're always worried about seeming sexist. They're also weird with each other: in Israel they hug each other, and spend lots of time together and call each other *achi*, my brother. Here they're always worried about people thinking they're a couple.

If Toronto ever feels too sterile, or too unfriendly, I try to tell myself I'm seeing more of the world. I like Queen Street West because I love to watch the people: stoned teenagers with patches for bands I've never heard of on their jackets, who walk around squinting in the bright sunlight, laughing as they stumble out of the McDonald's at Spadina; kids from the suburbs in jeans and sweatshirts who look giddy, their parents' credit cards and ten shopping bags in each hand; vegans with dreads who wear pentagrams or agate around their necks, who love the crystal shops and the shoe stores selling three-hundred-dollar non-leather boots. There's the fashionistas wearing six-inch heels and fur-trimmed coats who float in a cloud of designer perfume that always smells like a heady mix of amber musk and vanilla, and people with green or purple hair, full arms of colourful tattoos, and at least two face piercings, usually an eyebrow and their nose.

I love the way the buildings look worn out in individual ways, some with fading graffiti, some with boarded storefronts, like they each have a complex history that's waiting to be discovered. I love the different styles of architecture—in Israel a lot of low-rise buildings were built in the seventies and look identical to each other, paint peeling off the concrete the same ways. I love the coffee shops that seem to burst with creative people, musicians and writers and artists. There's a place near Bellwoods that makes great espresso shots. I go there at least three times a week when I work an afternoon shift.

I always talk to at least one person I find interesting: today it was a writer who was working on a play about a group of doctors. Two days ago, I met a cellist who was about to do a series of concerts in Hong Kong.

I love CDRR because it reminds me of a mix of a rock club I used to go to that was wedged between a tattoo parlour and a brothel on Bograshov Street in central Tel Aviv, and these arty bars I used to hang out in a part of South Tel Aviv called Florentine. Florentine is a mix of musicians, filmmakers and foreign workers. The rent is cheap and the buildings are decaying. It looks different, more underground and less commercial, but it feels a lot like Parkdale.

I love seeing bands play every night at CDRR. It was easier in Israel because I actually knew who the bands were and understood the connotations of their lyrics. I remember seeing the band Habiluim play in a tiny gallery with only fifty people, drinking and swaying, feeling like I was part of an inside joke of fun and social critique.

I never feel so connected in Toronto, but I love all the foreigners who stumble into CDRR. They're probably thinking of similar bars back home too. It's comforting to think that every big city in the world could have a similar underground culture. I like that about travelling: I just need to find the right street or area, and I can find my home.

Alon was five years older than me, which used to seem like a lot, when I wanted to go out and he always wanted to stay home. I met him right after the army. I moved back into my parents' apartment when I was done my service.

I slid neatly right back into my old life.

I didn't have to get a job at first. I hardly made any money being in the army, but it was enough that for the first two months I didn't have to do anything. I sat in my room, listening to music, trying to block out the oppressive Israeli sun. I was directionless and depressed. I didn't realize how much I appreciated the structure of army life. I didn't know what to do with the hours of freedom I suddenly had.

All my best friends went backpacking through South America, India and Thailand. I didn't see the point of all the trekking; it just seemed like an expensive distraction. What I wanted sometimes was a lobotomy, the kind of procedure that would make me want my own life, that would make me want to be the person my parents wanted me to be. Deep down I knew that I wasn't capable of being anything except myself, and if I wanted to do that, I'd have to strike out into the world completely on my own. The thought terrified me, so I spent most of my time for weeks sitting on the balcony or in the park near my building, getting high.

I met Alon at the pet store he worked in. I was being paid to watch the neighbour's cat while they went up north for the weekend. The cat was old, fourteen or so, with missing teeth. What he needed was this expensive canned cat food that I could only buy in a specialty pet store on a weird side-street blocks away. This despite the fact that there were probably at least five pet stores on Ahuza, our town's main street, that were much closer. I remember being so annoyed—this decrepit cat was getting in the way of my doing nothing.

I walked all the way there, and there he was, behind the counter. He had long hair, tied back in a ponytail, a hair band keeping stray pieces out of his eyes, and milky pale skin, with freckles. He was tall, almost a foot taller than me. His smile was friendly in an easy, casual way. I asked him for the cat food.

I don't know you, he said, looking me in the eye.

No, of course not, I answered. *Why would you?*

He laughed. *No, I just meant that I've never seen you in here before. We get the same people in here all the time.* He paused. *I think I would've remembered you.*

I smiled. A lot of Israeli men started up with women of any age and appearance, whether they were married or single, to flirt with them, or sleep with them, just for fun, and it often meant nothing at all. For some reason I believed him, or maybe it was just mutual attraction.

I described my middle-aged neighbours for him.

Yes, I know them. Then—*Eich korim lach*—what's your name?

Nili, I said, blushing. I was fat as a teenager, and even at twenty-one, years after I'd lost the weight, I was still caught off guard if a guy actually liked me.

I asked him his name. *Alon*, he said, which means an oak tree.

I'd never loved nature names, but when I looked into his hazel eyes and saw the earthy browns and greens, I thought, *Mamash matim lecha*, it really suits you.

I wrote my number down for him. He called me that night. On our first date he drove us to the Sharon beach, in Herzliya, a small city next to our town. He couldn't have known, but it was my favourite beach since I was a kid. The water was always the lightest shade of blue, and was never freezing cold, even in the winter. There was the famous part near the Marina that was always full of tourists and fancy boats, and there was the other stretch, full of piles of shells, and huge eroding stones that I'd always loved the most. It always felt more intimate.

It was Friday afternoon, and the sun was setting as we walked. The sea was tinged with orange. He held my hand. I walked around picking up shells.

He told me I was acting like a kid, getting excited about such tiny things, but he was smiling.

He told me about his life growing up on a kibbutz in the north. He described the green valleys and hills full of trees near where he grew up.

It must have been beautiful, I said, *growing up in nature like that.*

He nodded. *It was. But it was also scary, when we were kids, growing up so close to the Lebanon border.*

I took a photo of the inside of his hand, his fingers wrapped around one of mine. I took another one of his face, up close, the fading sun in his soft eyes. We were lying down together, away from the water. His hair was loose, almost the same colour as the sand. He was smiling.

He kissed me on the sand, peeled my clothes off, slowly, as the sky got darker. It was actually less romantic than it sounds—I got sand in uncomfortable places—but he loved it. *It's like we're part of the beach,* he said.

I smiled. *I like the way you think,* I said. I felt very calm around him.

We moved in together a few months later, into the tiny apartment he rented in Mikhmoret, a tiny beachside town about forty-five minutes away from Ra'anana. It was a place where people rented summer houses so it was dead quiet in winter. We lived near a beach that felt like it belonged to us.

I worked in a nearby café, and took a lot of photos, mainly portraits of people, especially when they weren't looking. I liked capturing spontaneous gestures.

My parents stopped talking to me. Their reasons were transparent: I was living with a guy I wasn't married to, having premarital sex. I wasn't pretending to be religious anymore;

he wasn't religious at all, he wasn't rich or ambitious, and had no interest in becoming any of those things. They didn't care about how kind he was, or how well he treated me.

He convinced me that I had to go with him to India, and we saved for months to travel—backpacked through India, from Delhi to Mumbai to Kerala, meeting Israelis everywhere we went. We saw the Taj Mahal and the Ganges, heard traditional Hindustani and Carnatic music live, stayed in hostels packed to the rafters with people of every culture, made amazing friends, bought tons of colourful scarves and thin, cotton clothes in markets, got sunburned, then beautifully browned. We got dysentery from bottled water that was really tap water—twice—ate mouthwatering curry and spicy vegetables and *chapati*, learned how to order in Hindi, ate chicken at McDonald's because they didn't serve beef, saw sacred cows, saw dirt roads and beautiful animals crossing them, did tons of drugs, smoking things I'd never heard of but still dream about, had Ayurvedic massages and saw tropical dry forests.

It was an amazing experience to have together, but it affected us differently. He had been to India before, and loved it, but was a little desensitized. I felt like I was awake for the first time in years. Seeing all the poverty broke my heart. The beauty contrasted with the kids, so many of them, sitting on street corners, begging, with huge eyes and outstretched, dirty palms.

Suddenly, I was so sure, I wanted to be a photographer, a journalist even. I realized I had to keep travelling, keep documenting things. I realized I wanted to study overseas, and I had to learn English. I wanted to travel more, save every shekel I had for it. I realized I had to move to Tel Aviv to get a better paying job, or it would never happen. I wanted to move to Canada or the US to study. I always knew I wanted to be an artist, but now I knew what kind.

My parents were surprisingly supportive. It was Alon who couldn't understand it—how I had been so happy with our life before but now I wanted to change everything. Why I couldn't just be happy with him, be satisfied with what we had.

I tried for months, but I couldn't do it. I wanted more. I also knew that I wanted to get married one day, and he'd always been against marriage. I knew that was unlikely to ever change.

Worse, Alon was starting to take drugs really seriously.

I really believe that acid expands your mind, he said to me in the kitchen, after he'd spent his whole day off doing hit after hit. I didn't know what to say to him.

I cried for months after we broke up. We broke up and got back together about five times before it finally stuck. I really loved him. I loved how comfortable he was in his own skin. I loved the confidence he had to just do whatever felt right to him. I loved the way he'd gaze at me across the table when we were eating, and I'd know that he loved me without him saying a word.

We hardly ever fought, but maybe that was the problem.

My friend Inbar said that it was unhealthy that we never wanted to talk about anything difficult. *Fighting is part of the passion*, she insisted.

I shrugged. I'd always loved how deeply calm Alon was. But if I did try to talk about serious things—and I did at the beginning of our relationship—he'd get this cold, dead, still-like-a-statue expression, and just refuse to have the conversation. Even if he woke up in the middle of the night sweating from a nightmare flashback about his time in the army, he wouldn't say much. He'd let me hold him or hug him and that was about it. He could be really stubborn sometimes.

Ein mah la'asot, I told Inbar, there was nothing to do.

Alon lives with his girlfriend now, in our old apartment. They have two dogs. He sends me photos of them, and their dogs, when I email him. She looks exactly like the kind of girl who's perfect for him—all hippie clothing, floor-sweeping dresses and Indian silk scarves. Her name is Neta, which means bud. A tree and a bud. It's nauseating. I know it's ridiculous to be jealous of her. I know I'm not supposed to miss him anymore, but I do. I've never really stopped, even though I am happier with the way my life is now.

I try to focus my thoughts on Lukas now. I try to push Alon out of my heart and out of my system. I go to the bar even though it's not my night to work and ask Dez to make me a drink. He makes me some Jagerbombs and we laugh, and talk shit. That's the thing I like about Dez—he's funny and he doesn't ask too many questions.

When I get home, stumbling over the pile of shoes at our door, Lukas is there, sitting on the couch.

I was waitin' for you, he says. He hugs me, and says he's sorry.

Things will be okay, I think, *it's possible.*

Lukas kisses me and in that moment, I think, *I believe you.*

Marlize

We're lying in bed. *What's it like,* I ask him, *where you're from?*

It's nice, he says. *It's got a lot of bars.*

I smile. *Like CDRR?*

Dez laughs. *No, not as cool.* He runs his fingers along my stomach. The heat is on full blast in the apartment, and it's as hot as Cape Town in February. I can't stop sweating, even in my bra and underwear. I pull off his t-shirt so he's just wearing white boxer briefs and lie on his chest.

I don't know, he says. *It's nice. We have a couple of soccer stadiums, and our teams are pretty good. We have two:* cruzeiro *and* atletico, *my team is* cruzeiro. *I mean, some people in Brazil call us* zebras, *but I don't know, we've been doing really well these last few seasons.*

Zebras? I ask.

Oh, yeah. It's what we call a team that we're sure is going to lose. Deu zebra. *I have no idea why, actually.*

I laugh. *I like it when you speak Portuguese,* I tell him. *It's kind of hot.*

He kisses me. *Você é belo e sexy,* he says. *You're beautiful and sexy.*

I try to repeat the words, the sounds, try to look him in the eye, because Dez is both of those things.

That's good, he says. *That's really good.* He kisses my neck.

No, tell me more about your city, I say. *We have to have conversation, sometimes,* I tell him. *I want to really get to know you.*

He grins. *Okay, conversation first, then sex.* I laugh, and nod.

Okay, he says. *We have a lot of universities and parks. There's a national park not too far away called* Mata do Jambreiro. *It's one of my favourite places in the world. You drive through it. It's the biggest forest I've ever seen, full of rosewood and cedar trees, I used to like to roll the windows down, and just sniff. It smelled like perfume. There were squirrels and monkeys swinging from trees. I saw an anteater there once. Have you ever seen one in real life?*

I try to think if I have.

They really snort ants, tons of them at once, like the most hard-core cokeheads I've ever seen. It's so funny. My mom and dad used to take us there when we were little kids. I wish you could see it, he says dreamily.

I nod. *Me too,* I say.

My city's surrounded by mountains on all sides. It's kind of weird for me, how flat Toronto is, you know?

Yeah, I say. *I do know. The layout of this city is too clean and easy, it's boring. All you have to do is memorize the names of intersections and you never get lost.*

He nods. *Which is good, if you're afraid of getting lost, like me.*

I look up at him and grin. *Seriously? You're afraid of getting lost?*

He sighs. *Okay. I got lost in a mall once, when I was a kid. It was like, childhood trauma or something.*

I start to laugh, then realize he's serious.

What, it was scary, he says, and I touch his face.

How old were you? I ask.

Five, he says, staring off, away from me. *It took my mom two hours to find me, and the first thing she did was slap me.*

I look up at him, take his hand. *Shame,* skat, I say.

He asks me what *skat* means, and I tell him it's what you call someone you care about, like sweetheart or honey. *I like it,* he says. *In Portuguese, we say* chuchu.

I feel shy all of a sudden, so I change the subject.

Cape Town's got a lot of mountains too. I tell him about Table Mountain, how deeply carved the stone is, how the top is so flat you could eat on it, how on overcast days the white clouds swirl over, like a tablecloth. I tell him about the game reserves, how you can see lions and their cubs up close. I tell him about Kloof Street, the main street downtown, that's full of boutiques bursting with local designer stuff, and little restaurants, and bars, so many bars. I tell him about Evol, the dance club on Hope Street I used to go to with my sister that played indie rock and alternative stuff. I tell him how the regulars dress there; I describe the skin-tight jeans, the thick eyeliner. I never felt cool enough when I went, so I stopped going. I tell him about playing pool with my friends at Stones, how no one ever asked you for ID if you were a girl. I tell him about the *bergies*, the homeless people who sit around, waiting to steal your cigarettes out of your hands, always asking me for money I never had. I smile.

I love how you always try to give money to homeless people, I tell him. The other night, we were walking down the street, and he stopped and gave a guy ten dollars. He spent ten minutes listening to the guy rant, before he realized we had to go.

I pull myself up, closer to him, trace his heart with my fingertips. He doesn't know how kind he is.

I tell him about the different beaches, how clear and salty the water was, how deep and shiny and turquoise, how in Simon's Town, the Atlantic and Indian Oceans meet. I tell him how my friends and I would go at night, take a bottle of red wine and sit talking, on the sand. I tell him about fire-throwing shows on one of the beaches at night, how magical it felt to watch them when you were a little drunk, how the oranges and reds blurred into the black sky, into the tiny glittering stars.

I tell him about the crime, the men who stand around waiting to rob people who used the bank machine near the Spar supermarket near my old house. I tell him how many security systems we had, how we had walls and barbed wire and a dog. How it wasn't enough.

I don't realize it but I'm crying. I tell him how much I miss my sister, my mother, how I never talk to my dad, and when I do, he's vacant, vague. I tell Dez how I feel like I've lost my dad too.

I miss my old life sometimes, I find myself saying. *I miss what it was, what it could've been. I miss being able to dance, knowing what my future was going to be, knowing exactly what I was good at. I miss feeling like a kid, feeling like I didn't have to be responsible for every choice and decision I made. I miss having a home.*

He puts both arms around me, he's holding me close.

Sometimes I wish you could protect me if I go back, I tell him. *I'm too afraid to go alone. But I miss it.*

I will, he tells me, over and over, stroking my hair.
Goodnight skat, he says, before I drift off.
Night chuchu, I whisper, and fall into a deep sleep.

Dez

We're in her little shoebox kitchen. I'm going to cook her dinner.

I want to make you something we eat in Belo Horizonte, I say. *Something you've never had before.* She seems excited.

I start making *feijoada,* a stew of beans, pork, beef, rice, and vegetables. I cleaned out the kitchen at work, because I want to impress her.

People eat it all over Brazil, I say, *but in my city, we add slices of orange.*

I cook the rice, add black beans, and start chopping up onions and garlic. I find a dirty spoon, wipe it with hand sanitizer that I have in my pocket, and give her a sample. She rocks back and forth on her toes, does a little dance of two or three springing steps.

Amazing, she says. *I likeee.* She's always teasing me about my accent, the way I sometimes add 'ee's to the ends of words that are silent in English.

I stick out my bottom lip, try to look down like she's hurt my feelings but we both start laughing.

You're so cute, she says, glides over to me and kisses me. *I loveee your accent.*

I have to concentrate so she steps back, sits on one of those dark wood country chairs that look fancier than anything a student could own. *Nice chairs,* I say.

They belong to my roommate's mom, she says.

The sink is piled full of dirty plates, pots, knives, spoons and filthy sponges. A roach crawls out of the garbage can.

I'm really glad Marlize isn't kitchen staff at the club.

She catches me staring at it, then wrinkles her nose in the way she knows I find adorable.

She blames her roommate, says she hates the mess, the smell in here too. Says she's given up trying to do it for her, she has to learn on her own. I have no idea whether Marlize is lying or not, but it's cute that she cares.

She invites me to sit down with her, but I'm okay where I am, leaning with my back against the counter, shoulders grazing against the glass cabinets, filled with plastic glasses and plates from Honest Ed's.

Something heavy is coming.

There are things I need to know about you, she says.

I don't want to show her that I'm sweating, that I'm worried about what she might ask, so I look her in the eye and say, *You can ask me anything. I'll tell you anything.*

Okay, she says, and takes a deep breath. My heart feels like it is crushing my ribcage.

Why does everyone call you Dez?

I'm so relieved I start laughing hysterically. That's the serious question she wants answered?

I could live with this, I think. *I could live with this girl.*

Oh, it was a nickname from high school, from soccer. Leonardo's a pretty common name in Brazil; there were three of us in my class. They had to have something to print on the back of our jerseys. Da Silva is pretty common too. I think my dad came up with it, actually. I asked him to think of something that was cool, and short. He came up with it in about a second. He was so cool, my dad.

She lays her hand on my arm. *You must really miss him*, she says.

I sigh. *I do, yeah. All the time. My mom and I got along much better when he was around. She started expecting so much from me after he died. I think that a big part of why I left was to get away from that. Does that sound horrible?*

She shakes her head. *No, I had to get away from my dad too, from my grandparents. Everyone expected me to fill the hole that my mother and sister left, and all I wanted to do was be alone. All I wanted to do was tell everyone to fuck off. All I wanted was the space and time to figure out what I wanted, then to be allowed to do it.*

I lean down, kiss her softly. *That's it, exactly*, I say. It's crazy how well she can articulate what I'm feeling.

She looks up at me, eyes focused on my lips like she's about to kiss me. *There's something else I have to ask you*, she says.

Shoot. I love that expression. It took me ages to figure out how to use it properly. I tell her that, and she laughs.

You know what we say in South Africa? Shot, *instead of shoot. We also say it like thank you. Like if you bought me a drink. I could say,* shot, *babe.*

That's cute, I say, and kiss her. *Mmm* shot chuchu, she murmurs, and giggles.

I keep kissing her, harder and deeper, but she pulls away suddenly and looks serious again.

Are you involved with Nicki too? Or have you been? I've noticed you guys talking a lot lately and I was wondering. Do you usually do this?

I started laughing again. *No,* I said. *Really. I've never even thought of Nicki that way. I don't know why, but I haven't. It never occurred to me. I mean, she's cool, but I'm not attracted to her at all.*

The muscles in her arms start to relax, and her expression changes.

Really? she asks.

Really. I promise. And it is *different,* I tell her. *I don't know why, but it is. I feel different with you than I've felt with anyone in a long time, maybe ever. I feel like we're friends, me and you. Like there's the other stuff*—she smiles and nods—*but, like, I can really talk to you.*

She nods again, and kisses me, grabs my ass and then leads me to the bedroom. I never do finish making dinner.

It feels strange, for once, being honest with a girl. It feels strange for once to feel a little bit vulnerable.

Nicki

I'm at a coffee place at Queen and Bathurst today when I see a sign about a rally at Queen's Park.

It's to protest the genocide in Gaza. They quote Naomi Klein and Noam Chomsky, people I admire and respect who compare it to Apartheid in South Africa or the Holocaust.

I feel a deep pit of shame forming in my stomach. I really want to go.

I've been raised my whole life to think of the Arabs in Israel as the enemy, to fear them bombing the shit out of us. I've had my car randomly checked at security points, had my handbag emptied at mall entrances to check for weapons. I've learned to fire a gun in basic army training. I've learned to put on and breathe through a gas mask from the time I was ten. I've learned to run down to the bomb shelter in the basement of my building in thirty seconds or less, and I lived on the fifth floor.

I've lived a life based on fear, and if you're afraid and feel threatened, you instinctively strike back.

But what if I've been wrong? What if most of them just want peace? Away from Israeli propaganda for the last few years, I've been able to really think about everything for the first time.

I watch the attacks on Gaza on Canadian TV, horrified to see little kids get killed, and hospitals get blown to shit. There's blood and bits of skin everywhere the cameras pan—like the bus bombings or pizza parlour bombings in Jerusalem but on a way bigger scale. We have the army power, the soldier power that they don't have. I cry when I watch it, see the scenes in my nightmares. That's what I fought in the army for? That's the kind of victory my people are killing for?

The words *Am Yisrael Hai* are spray-painted onto buildings in South Tel Aviv: *The Nation of Israel Lives.* Before I left, someone added *yalim* on some of them, so that it read *Am Yisrael Haiyalim. The Nation of Israel Are Soldiers.*

And for what? So we can inflict suffering on a people as

scared and innocent and brainwashed and fucked up and as possessive of the land and culture as we are?

I want to go—I want to see who the people are who go to these things. I want to talk to them and understand things a little bit better. I want an outlet for this anger I've been shoving down and ignoring for so long. I want to understand myself, why I did things for so long that I didn't agree with or believe in.

I knew a guy, a friend of a friend who jumped through the army psychiatrist's ground floor window in the middle of the interview. He landed in a bush, brushed himself off, and left. Needless to say, the army didn't want him. I knew a girl who told the shrink she heard planes flying over her parents' house at night and was terrified they'd crash into her bedroom. She got points for creativity for sure. I had another friend, Smadar, who tried to convince them that she was opposed to the army for moral reasons. Apparently, they grilled her three times in a tiny room, asked her so many questions that she was forced to give up and plead insanity to get out of it.

I was technically from a religious enough family to get out of the army. Religious women in Israel got to do a year of volunteering called National Service instead, but my family wouldn't have it. I hadn't been near a synagogue in years, so I guess they thought it would straighten me out or something. My dad went on and on about what an honour it was to fight for Israel; my mom was relieved that I'd be mostly in an office on an army base near Tel Aviv. Being in Intelligence, I wasn't allowed to talk about my job at the time and I guess I never did.

Still, I wonder now why I did it, and if I did the right thing. I wonder how my life would be now if I hadn't gone. Would I be happier with myself?

I want to go home one day to a country that's not always at war with itself.

Dez

Marlize never wants to talk about the night she was attacked. Aside from telling me about it that one night, in the bar, before we even started seeing each other, she hardly ever mentions it. We've been spending most nights together lately, at my house or at her apartment and I'm a heavy sleeper, so at first I didn't notice it, but after waking up to go the bathroom last week, I realize that she suffers from serious nightmares.

She mumbles and screams in her sleep, mostly in Afrikaans. She kicks and flails violently, her long fingers balled into fists. Last night she slapped me on the shoulder so hard that it hurt. When she wakes up, practically swimming in her own sweat, she looks dazed. She obviously has no idea that it's happening.

Is okay, I tell her. *Is okay* meu amor, I say over and over, until she calms down. I have no idea what else to say. Sometimes if she lets me, I hold her. I rub her back and ask her if she wants to talk, and she usually doesn't.

Tonight, when she wakes up, at around 3:00 a.m., she tells me for the first time about her sister Claudette. Marlize is irritated, she says, because she's still getting emails from acquaintances and former classmates, telling her how sorry they are about Claudette's death.

Isn't it nice that people still care? I ask her.

She sighs. *At first it was nice,* she says. *But after a while, it becomes really grating. It's strange when people you don't know, who barely knew her, are telling you how wonderful she was. Nobody knew her like I did. If they think it's hard for them, they should just imagine what the loss was like for me. I've known her since I was born.*

I know, I say, *I know. Of course it's harder for you.*

She looks at me. *Did I ever tell you what she was like,* she asks me.

I shake my head. *No, not at all. What was she like?*

She smiles, looks dreamily at the wall like she's seeing something else. *My sister was the kind of girl who'd always give you her opinion without holding back.*

I laugh. *Sounds like my sisters, Thais and Isabella.*

She squeezes my hand. *How come you never talk about them?*

I shrug. *There isn't so much to say. We live very different lifestyles. They live with their families in Belo Horizonte. We Skype about once a week, a few minutes here and there. I think the distance is ideal. It helps me feel less guilty. We feel each other's love but not each other's judgement, you know? It's better.*

She smiles then looks sad. *Tell me more about your sister*, I say.

She always wanted to figure out what the truth was, and to say it out loud as many times as possible, to anyone who would listen to her. She had no sense of privacy. She was honest where I held back, loud and impulsive where I was careful. She always took risks—a lot of them were stupid, but some of them were really inspiring.

What did she do that was inspiring? I ask.

She was a film student, she says. *But she was already getting paid to make documentaries. I heard my dad tell someone at the funeral that he's sure she would have become an important filmmaker. I'd always thought so, too.*

She was working on a documentary on the people of Mitchell's Plain, the mixed-race township of Cape Town that was called District Six in the 1970s. She interviewed people on the street, became friends with them and was invited into their homes, to speak to their families. She spoke to them about the crime there, about gangster warfare and teenage pregnancies. The massive problem there was methamphetamine addiction, a drug the locals called tik. *She talked to addicts and their partners, mothers and kids about why it happened to the one they loved. She really wanted to understand. Claudette suffered from depression and took medication to control it. She had empathy for people's pain—she was always giving money to street kids, talking about how her and Tshepo were going to adopt one day instead of having their own kids.* There's too many beautiful children who don't have loving homes, *she'd tell me.* There's too many people in this country as it is. Why should we add to the numbers? *My mom would be beside herself—sweating, and pacing back and forth in the kitchen every time Claudette had to go there. Nothing ever happened to her. She had amazing luck. She'd never been mugged or had her cell phone stolen.*

What did she look like, I ask her. *Did you guys look alike?*

Not really, she says. *We had different features, different body types. There was some resemblance, a little bit anyway, but we didn't really look like sisters. She had a prettier face than me,* she says, and I shake my head.

I don't believe it, I say, *you're beautiful. The most beautiful.*

She laughs, and gives me a kiss. *No, it's true,* she insists. *She did. Her face was round, with a widow's peak and a high forehead. She had green eyes and a huge, open smile. She wasn't thin, but she wasn't fat. When you hugged her, her body felt nicely padded. She always wore loose-fitting clothes, peasant blouses and caftans, floor-length skirts and long-sleeved dresses. She wore scarves all year round, even in summer. She had rain boots with flowers— huge orange Proteas—hand-painted on them that she wore every day in winter.*

When I went through her stuff after she died, I grabbed a handful of her scarves and one of her cameras to keep. You know that scarf, the maroon and white tie-dyed one? I nod. She'd been wearing it earlier. Before we went to bed, I'd used it to tie her up. She was more into it than I expected.

It used to be Claudette's. She bought it in an outdoor market on a trip to Angola. I wear it when I miss her the most. Sometimes I use her camera and take pictures of people or places in Toronto. I don't know if I have her talent, or her eye, but it feels comforting.

I want to see your photos sometime, I tell her. She looks away, suddenly shy.

I want to take some photos of you sometime, she says.

I laugh and look down. We're both naked. *I want to take some photos of you too,* I tell her. She actually blushes.

I meant of your face, she says, and touches the top of my cheek, below my eye.

I smile. *Okay,* I say. *You can take one anytime.*

Even tonight, she asks. I nod.

Before we go to bed, or tomorrow. Whatever you prefer.

She points to a chain on her neck. *Did I tell you about this?* I shake my head. *Before I left, my dad gave me my mom's wedding band. It was too big for my finger, so I wear it like this. My mom and I always lived in our own separate worlds, but we both knew that we loved each other. I'm sad, when I think about it sometimes, not about what I lost, but what we could've had. We could've had more time to spend together. My mom and I were both reserved, kind of the same you know? I could've tried much harder. We could have understood each other better. We could've been so much closer.*

I hold her close, and she presses her face into my neck as she cries.

Is that what you dream about at night? I ask her.

No, she says. *I dream about the attack, but this time I'm fighting back. This time I'm not a sheltered girl in shock. This time I bliksem them, and even if I die, I don't just sit there frozen, I scream and I fight and I try.* She shakes her head. *Do you know what it's like? To live in a place where you don't feel safe? Where your own home feels like a prison, and you can't walk alone at night?*

I nod. *Uai, I'm from Brazil, babe. There's a lot of crime there too. I think it's worse if you're a woman.*

Like in South Africa?

I think so. What you were saying about Claudette, and the street children? There's a lot of them in Belo Horizonte too. They wait at traffic lights and go up to cars when they stop, when it's red. It's very sad. People get mugged there all the time. I got mugged once, nothing serious, just a guy came up to me at an ATM with a knife, so I emptied out my chequing account. It was no big deal. I didn't have much in it. People there never walk around with wallets, just a credit card and a little more cash than you need for the night, just in your pocket. You always walk with two amounts, you know? Keep them in different pockets so that if you get mugged, you can give them the smaller pile. People get attacked sometimes. There's drug crime, and kidnappings can happen there. It's a different world. But I do understand. I didn't even realize how often I didn't feel safe there until I moved here.

I look down at her. *Do you ever keep up with what's happening at home? It's like I can't anymore, the news in Brazil are too depressing.*

She smiles. *It's weird that we say the news* is, *instead of* are.

I groan. *You have to help me with my English, it's embarrassing.*

She kisses my cheek. *Your English is great.* She pauses. *And no, I never watch South African news. I find it scary.*

I stroke her hair. *You're protected here,* I tell her. *You're safe.*

With you, she asks.

Yeah, with me. But safeguarded in general, in Canada. It's a much better life here, querida, *given what we both know. We'll be sheltered here.*

You think so? she asks.

I know so, I tell her. I let her take a photo of me before we drift off. It's of my face and neck, up to my shoulders. *You have a good eye,* I tell her. She really does. It's a great shot.

Dez, she asks me, leans into me with her back before she drifts off. *How do you say, I like you, in Portuguese?*

Gosto de você, I say. *But I don't think it's such a great expression. I like* paixao da minha vida *more. It means passion of my life. That's better isn't it?*

She rolls over to face me, kisses me and repeats it.

Good pronunciation, I say. It really was. *I have another one for you,* I tell her, before she falls asleep. *Minha alma é sua, e meu corpo também. It means my soul belongs to you, and my body too,* I whisper.

She smiles, but I'm not sure if she heard me. Part of me hopes she didn't. I've possibly never meant those words before. It's weird to worry so much about what she thinks. It's a little disarming.

Lukas

Nicki keeps askin' me what I think about politics. Today she shows me a translated article from *Ha'aretz*, which she says is Israel's leftist paper.

Look at the way we've mistreated the Palestinians, she says, her voice cracking with passion. It confuses me. I don't even have a basic understanding and to be honest, I don't want to. I can tell I'm frustrating her, standin' there, sayin' nothin' at all. She's always tryin' to find out what I really think.

I don't wanna pretend to believe in anything more than I really do. You put your name on a piece of paper, you check a box or put an X next to something, you put time and thought into your choice, and it doesn't turn out the way it's supposed to anyway. It never does. Protests and politics seem like such a waste of time to me.

My family never talked about that stuff, they just all voted separately. My mom used to vote Liberal. It was the most neutral choice if you were going to vote, the easiest thing. Both my father and my stepdad voted Conservative, because they always promised to spend the most on the military, and they were both military guys.

Good solid values, my stepdad would say, the day after he voted. *They're the only ones with their priorities in order.*

My stepbrother, when he studied at the technical college down in Halifax, voted NDP 'cause they promised to lower tuition fees. He started voting for the Green Party when he graduated, right before I went into juvie. He had his own landscaping company, all earth-friendly. Recycling became his politics. I used to get so bored havin' to listen to him talk.

Some of Nicki's artist friends she knows from work talk to her about how bad the Conservative government is, how they want to cancel arts funding and how they want to protest. She thinks it's fantastic.

Why can't you care, she asks me. *This is your country we're talking about.* I don't know what to tell her. I'm twenty-five and I've never voted in my life.

Last night she comes home from work talkin' about what Marlize said about the corrupt South African government. How millions of their currency there, rands they're called, disappear each year, and then the politicians show up, drivin' fancy cars, wearin' designer clothes.

The crime gets worse, she tells me. *They have the highest murder rates in the world, not to mention rape and HIV. I don't understand*, she says, tears forming in her eyes, *what's wrong with the world.*

I don't know what to tell her. *It's fucked*, I say. *The world is fucked.* I don't know what else to say.

People just live their lives here, she says. *They go to Queen Street, go to work, go home, get laid, worry about stupid shit like whether their partner actually loves them—meanwhile the world is fucking falling apart—and their lives just go on. You know? Marlize was telling us about her neighbour who got gang-raped for going to a party on a Saturday night. Her other friend got beaten up and robbed just for using a bank machine—and the world in Toronto just keeps on turning. Soldiers in Israel get tortured and killed, innocent Israeli and Palestinian kids get blown to shit for eating pizza on the patio of a restaurant, or going to the fucking market, or walking down the street, and we're here in Toronto—* she's hysterical now, cryin', shakin'—*trying to decide between buying a Black Flag or Joy Division t-shirt at an overpriced music store, between a soy latte or a fucking bubble tea.*

There's a snot bubble coming out of her nose when she's sayin' this, and I try not to laugh, I try but I fail, and then she's angry, she's still cryin', she starts screamin', *Don't laugh at me, don't fucking laugh at me, you never understand anything.* Then she's yellin', yellin' in Hebrew now, I don't know what she's sayin', but she's so angry, she shoves me.

She's surprisingly strong, and her leg makes contact with my shin. She kicks me, she kicks me and it hurts, shoves me again, slaps my neck just below my chin, and that's it, I've had it.

I hit her back.

I aim for her shoulder, gonna get a good punch in, but she ducks, and I miss. I sock her in the jaw. She crumples to the floor, she's quiet, holding her face, lookin' at me with those huge eyes, and all I can think is, *I hit my girlfriend, fuckin' hell, I got her good.*

She gets up all slow, and then she's backin' away from me, into the kitchen, I'm standin' in the living room all dazed. She gets an ice pack for her chin, the skin already gettin' darker.

When I hit her it didn't feel that hard. I'm capable of worse, but I guess you never actually know until you inflict pain.

We don't talk for what feels like hours.

Later that night, she gets into bed with me. I put my arms around her.

I say, *I'm sorry I'm sorry I'm sorry*, a million times.

It's okay, she says. *I deserved it, I hit you first.*

You don't deserve it, I say, but she looks me in the eye, all serious, like she means it.

Today, she stares into the mirror, sees the purple splotch forming on her little chin, and says, *I saw this movie at work on a Tuesday, you know how they show movies sometimes, upstairs, about a guy who hits a girl, during, you know, sex, and she likes it, she asks for it. It could be kind of fun, maybe? Maybe later, tonight, when we're messing around, you could hit me, maybe somewhere people can't see, but it could be fun.* Her eyes are all lit up, she's starin' at me, smilin' a little. She's serious I think.

I can't answer. I'm backin' away, walkin' backwards til I reach the door, til I reach my coat. I grab it, check my wallet's in my back pocket, and run, run, run, up the street, down Queen, away from her.

She's not following me. I keep running though, til it's hard to breathe and I'm sweating. When I get to the corner of Gladstone I collapse, sit down on the damp sidewalk outside the club door. I haven't been here in months because she loves it here so much. I fuckin' hate it that she works here. I fuckin' hate all these greasy fuckin' people and their influence on her.

I see that clown Dez takin' out the garbage. He's friendly, which actually makes it worse.

Hey man, you looking for Nicki? She's got the night off tonight.

I get right up in his face, standin' over him, which isn't hard because I'm half a foot taller and twice as wide as him.

I know that, fucker. I always know where she is. I just came here to tell you to leave her the fuck alone.

What? What are you talking about, man?

You and all the degenerates who come here, Marlize, all the girls, the drugs, the movies. Do you know what you're doin' to her?

I grab him by the scruff of his neck. *You're ruining her. She's sweet and she's good, and this place is ruining her.*

He shakes and tries to loosen my grip. He looks like a rat caught in a trap.

Hey man, that's enough. Come on, don't make me call the cops.

I let go. I try to throw a quick punch to his jaw but he ducks and I get his left shoulder instead. He winces. He takes his phone out of his pocket.

I'm serious, man, I'll call the cops right now if you don't get out of here.

For a second I consider getting arrested. It would be so much easier to just get locked up, but I step back and he starts to walk inside.

She's too good for this place, I yell before he's gone.

She's too good for you, man, he says.

I can't even argue because it's true.

When I get home she's sittin' there waitin' for me on the couch.

I'm a fuckin' psychopath, I want to tell her. *You don't even know what I'm capable of. You wanna share my world so badly you'll let me hit you during sex. I shouldn't be anywhere near you. I shouldn't be near humankind.*

But I say nothin' like that. I never wanna say anything that would hurt her. I just tell her I love her, and I tell her I'm sorry.

She nods like she wants to believe me.

Nicki

I think a lot about the rally. It keeps my problems with Lukas further from my mind. I decide I need two days off, one to get ready and one for the actual day, and decide to ask Dez during a lull in one of my shifts. It's about five in the afternoon, and I find him in the back of the kitchen making out with Marlize. She's sitting on one of the granite counters with her legs wrapped around his waist. Her hair is loose and he's running his hands through it. For what feels like five minutes they don't even notice me. I cough.

So, you guys come here a lot? Marlize jumps down and blushes.

Um, hi, Nicki, Dez says and laughs. *Well, lately we have been. You'd think getting to see each other all day would be enough, but sometimes in the middle of the day I just have to kiss my girl, you know?*

Marlize looks happier than I've ever seen her look. She gives him a quick kiss and says she's going back out on the floor. She pats my arm on the way out. *See you soon, Nicki,* she says and smiles.

It's funny, I did notice her wearing makeup, and tying her shirts up to show her abs lately. She's also been friendlier. I guess it makes sense.

I turn to Dez in amazement. *Wow, I had no idea this was becoming a real thing,* I say.

He nods and laughs like he's equally surprised. *Yeah, I think so.*

That's nice, I say, *I'm happy for you guys.* I give him a hug.

I ask him for the days off, knowing that he'll probably say yes to anything.

He asks me how things are with Lukas, which I don't expect at all. I don't feel like answering honestly but I also don't have the energy to lie to him. I shrug and say, *Things are okay.*

He gives me a hug. *I want you to be happy too,* he says.

I ask him if I can take a smoke break, and I stand outside in the graffiti and piss-soaked alley, crying by the dumpsters.

I spend the next morning obsessing about what to wear to the rally. I decide on baggy clothes, cargo pants and a black sweater. I want to blend in. I wear a scarf around my neck that I bought in Shuk HaCarmel, the Carmel Market in Tel Aviv, that looks vaguely like a *keffiyeh*, a Palestinian scarf. My mother eyed me suspiciously when I bought it, but it was just about fashion then. I try not to think about it.

If people ask me where I'm from, I don't know what I'll say. People have mistaken me for being French before, so maybe that's what I'll say. I Google "France," read about the wine and cheese and music. I decide to say I'm from Bordeaux. It seems safer than saying I'm from Paris, because I've never been, and if other people have, and ask me questions, I'll look like an idiot. I figure there'll be less chance of running into people that know Bordeaux well.

When I get there, I meet a bunch of Canadians; university students, girls and guys.

They're so eager, giving me statistics, showing me internet photos of injured kids, apartment buildings smashed to rubble.

The Israelis violate basic human rights, a guy says, his eyes wet, and it's hard to disagree. He shows me a picture of a little girl, bleeding to death on the ground while her family waits in vain for an ambulance. I think of the Hebrew expression *ayom venora*, meaning truly terrible, a phrase that comes from the Torah. It never felt more apt. The sky is dark in the photo. It looks like it might rain blood.

I meet girls around my age from Saudi Arabia and Egypt and Syria. I meet a girl from Qalqilya, a Palestinian city so close to my town, I try not to laugh. When we worry about suicide bombers making their way in, it's through her city. It's a surreal moment. Her name is Doa, and she has huge brown eyes. She looks so innocent. Her whole body is covered except her hands and face. Her expression is serene. I suddenly want to hug her, want to be her friend.

When they ask me what religion I am, I find myself saying I'm Christian. I don't mean to lie; the words are out before I can stop myself. They don't ask me any more about it than that.

They tell me instead about Islam, about finding time to pray five times a day, about not being objectified by random guys on the street because they're all covered up. I have to admit that it sounds good. Israeli guys hit on anyone—it's not even a compliment. Seriously, all you have to have in Israel is a pulse.

I remember meeting a Jewish girl in Canada who told me she went to Israel knowing only two Hebrew expressions: *Ani nesua*, I'm married, for the ones who wouldn't leave her alone, and *Ani lo loveshet takhtonim*, I'm not wearing any underwear, in case she ever needed any help with anything. Apparently, she didn't have to lift her suitcase the entire time she was there.

I can't imagine what it would be like not to be harassed everywhere you go—from the kiosk to the supermarket to the coffee shop. It might be nice.

The men in Egypt are really respectful to woman, one girl tells me. *They hold open doors, they're polite.*

I try to imagine what that's like.

Another girl, Ruba, tells me about Muslim holidays, from Ramadan to Eid. Her face is animated, and her words pour out in long excited paragraphs. She describes the food and preparations they make, the special clothing they wear.

It's incredible. I listen, amazed that I could have gone this long without knowing anything about any of it.

There are more than one billion of us, one of them tells me. I'm incredulous. I want to learn. At the end of the day, Ruba tells me that she wants me to meet her brother, Malik.

Their family is powerful, she implies. Their father is an advisor to the king. They've travelled the world, but they've never been to Bordeaux. Or Israel, I bet.

I have a boyfriend, I find myself explaining to her.

Oh, don't worry, I just meant as a friend. You should come out with us and a bunch of our friends. Everyone would love you.

I wonder what my mother would say if she knew.

I wonder what Ruba's brother would say if he knew I was Israeli.

I wonder if I'll be able to tell him.

Mostly, I wonder what Lukas will think when he hears about this. I decide that it's better not to tell him.

Marlize

We're walking up Queen Street after a night out together. Dez wanted to take me on a real date; he's been really into that lately. Two nights before, we go for Vietnamese food in Chinatown, crunching on tantalizing chicken and cashews and carrots and greens dripping in lemongrass sauce, and star anise ice cream for dessert, then see some metal bands play upstairs at the El Mocambo. He buys me some ear plugs at the Smoke and Variety store next to it before.

Trust me, he says, and I do. My ears are still ringing after, but it's worth it. He's made my life so fun and exciting.

Do you know, the guy who used to book this place once booked the Rolling Stones here, years and years ago, he says. I shake my head. I don't.

I like Toronto's history, I say, and he laughs.

Me too.

We see a movie at the theatre at Richmond and John. It has huge seats with tons of leg room and food that costs more than the movie. Dez buys us popcorn and New York Fries and I drink a Diet Coke the size of his arm. It's a Will Ferrell movie; I'm not sure if I'll like it but I end up laughing a lot, mostly because of the smile on Dez's face, the little boy glee in his eyes.

I really love this guy, he says. I move in closer to him, sit with my head on his shoulder, give his neck a kiss. I love his laugh—deep in the throat, kind of loud, full of joy. He's not self-conscious when he laughs, he's totally in the moment.

It makes me happy, seeing him like this. *I love your laugh*, I tell him.

I love you, Marli, he says. *I really do.*

We see a folk act play at the Horseshoe after. He buys me glass after glass of whatever is on tap, Miller, I think. We stagger out at 1:00 a.m., arms around each other.

I love the spring, he says, smiling, and I laugh. He points out the tiny green buds starting to blossom on the trees on College Street.

We start to walk back to his place, and then decide to take a cab when we get to Bathurst. We make out in the backseat and the driver shakes his head.

So many couples get crazy in my car, he says. *I don't know what it is.*

Dez and I look at each other and laugh.

We get out, walk up his steps and see someone standing in front of his door, waiting for him.

I can make out her profile in the dim lighting, see how small and thin she is, how determined her stance is. Her hands are on her hips. He drops my hand. He opens his door, and turns the light on, and I can see the fear in his face, around his eyes, the way his lips are pursed. She looks right at him, ignores me. She has long dark hair, an aristocratic nose and thin lips, painted bright red, a scathing glare. She's beautiful and scary. They're speaking Portuguese, really fast—she's screaming before long.

I stand frozen just behind Dez. I wait for her to take a breath, for him to stop responding, and I grab his arm, pull him aside.

What's going on, I say, as quietly as I can. *Who is she?*

She looks at me, and smiles, and takes a step in my direction. *That's right*, she says, *we haven't met before, have we? I'm Adriana.*

I nod. *Hi, I'm Mar*—I start to say, but she interrupts me.

Oh, I know who you are. We employ you at CDRR. I'm his wife. For a second I think I've misheard her, but she repeats it. *Let me guess: Leonardo says he's in love with you.*

I take a deep breath and try not vomit. I try to stand but I feel like the floor's going to give way underneath me. I look at her. *What? I didn't know, he didn't tell me, I didn't know, really.*

She smiles. *Oh, I know. Leonardo never tells the girls he's involved with anything. But you should know. We've been married for seven years. See this house you like to visit? I own half of it. The business? I co-own that too.*

I'm too confused to even be angry. *How did you know I'd be here?* I ask her.

Oh, I didn't, she says. *I came to talk to him about the bar, about business models, marketing, some strategies. When he wasn't here I decided to wait for him. I thought something like this was going on,* she says, and looks at me like she's wondering what Dez could've seen in me. *I knew it couldn't be serious,* she says. *How old are you?* she asks.

Twenty-two, I say, not looking at her.

Leonardo, she says, like his name leaves a bad taste in her mouth. She shakes her head.

I look over at him for the first time. He hasn't said a word, hasn't made a sound. His eyes are pleading.

I have to go, I say. I know I can get a taxi in a second once I get back to Queen Street.

Marli, no, Dez yelps, his voice getting louder with each syllable. *Don't go. Please, don't go.*

I only look back twice. He's still looking at me both times, like in a movie. His eyes are beautiful, intense, like always. I only start crying when I finally get into a cab. I don't stop for hours.

I get home and get into bed.

I had trusted him. I believed everything he told me. But he hasn't actually told me anything about himself. I don't know him at all.

I stop talking to him, stop taking his calls, stop answering my phone and my door.

I stay in bed for days. A week and a half later, I realize that I'm pregnant.

Nicki

He's over six feet tall, with immense shoulders, even broader than Lukas, with a more assured swagger in his hips. He has espresso-coloured skin and caramel eyes, full lips and white picket-fence teeth. He has a puffy black afro with a comb sticking out of the back. He wears a bright yellow t-shirt, skinny red jeans and cobalt blue zip-up sweatshirt. He looks like Superman.

He bounds over, extending a large hand. *Hi, I'm Malik*, he says. *I hear you know my sister.*

I suddenly feel shy, stare at my shoes. *I like your name*, I say, smiling, trying to look up at him without blushing.

It means king, he says. I marvel at the similarity in our languages—*Melech* in Hebrew, *Malik* in Arabic. I say nothing of course.

I hear you're from France, he says. I nod. *I love Paris.*

I smile, afraid to say anything that would give me away.

He takes my hand. *Saudi Arabia is a romantic place too.*

Which city are you guys from, I ask.

Jiddah, he says.

Is it a big city?

Oh, yeah, it's huge. Millions of people. It's different from the rest of the country, more cosmopolitan. Lots of businesses and museums and festivals. More scenic than Toronto though. We have beautiful beaches, and the biggest fountain in the world. Nicer than the CN Tower for sure.

I laugh.

Plus, we have better stores. We have this place, Tahlia Street, that's way better than Yorkville for designer stuff, you know Burberry, Prada, all that.

I shrug. *Not really my thing*, I say. *When I go into stores in Yorkville, they always look at me like I'm about to shoplift. They practically follow me around the store. And I mean, they're right. Not that I'd shoplift, but that I obviously can't afford to shop there.*

He bends down so he can look me in the eye. *You just need a nice guy to take care of you*, he says, and I try not to smirk. I have no idea what to say to that.

He calls me the day after we meet. I happen not to be working that day, and Lukas hasn't been home in a day and a half. Malik asks me if I can be ready in an hour and I say I can. He picks me up in a silver car. I think it might be a Mercedes. He's was playing hip hop—Jay-Z's *The Black Album*. At least he has good taste in music. When we stop at a red light he leans over and gives me a lingering kiss on the cheek. There's something about this guy that makes me feel like a giddy sixteen-year-old. He oozes charm without seeming to try at all.

He wants to go to Starbucks for coffee, but I offer to take him somewhere in Kensington Market instead. It's one of those hole-in-the-wall free trade coffee places that smells like patchouli and sandalwood and has tea and coffee from countries I dream about visiting. Bob Marley's "Redemption Song" is playing as we walk in. Malik's eyes widen.

I love this place, he says, excited like a five-year-old. *Thank you so much for bringing me here.* It's the end of April, and warm enough to sit outside on their wooden patio.

I order jasmine tea, and he gets coffee. He orders us barbecued tofu and avocado sandwiches and sugary carrot cake with thick frosting. He insists on paying for everything.

He tells me how his city is a gateway to Mecca, the holy city that Muslims from all over the world visit at least once in their lives. He tells me all about *Hajj*, the holy pilgrimage that happens once a year in Mecca, how millions of Muslims from all over the world fill the city to celebrate.

Everyone, no matter how much money they have, or don't have, wears the same thing—these white sheets, tied in the waist, with sandals. You can't shave or wear perfume, or do anything superficial. It's incredible, he says, *you feel this incredible sense of unity with everyone around you. Everyone is the same, no matter what their background is. We're all just there to serve God and be forgiven for all the things we've done. I wish you could see it.*

Me too, I say. He tells me about Medina, the burial place of the prophet Muhammad, about the green-domed mosques, and the wide, open, stone courtyards, the beauty and the guilt he feels at not connecting more, at not feeling what he's supposed to feel.

I want so badly to tell him I understand, that I know exactly what he means, that I feel the same way when I go to Jerusalem, or Tsfat, but I can't. I am too afraid to. I pat his arm, and listen.

I wish you could come with me to see it one day, he says. *I feel like you understand me.*

I'd like that, I say, and then his expression changes like a thought is dawning on him.

But you're not Muslim, are you, he says. I shake my head. *You're Christian, right?*

Again, I nod, but I'm starting to feel silly. *I should just tell him I'm Jewish, and Israeli*, I think. He's an open-minded guy. I'm being ridiculous.

We walk around the market. He buys some hip hop on vinyl; I buy a vintage dress and some sunglasses. He holds my hand as we walk through. I stop to give some change to a homeless girl with neon blue dreads, and a pierced chin. He gives her a dollar.

You know, according to Muslim culture, a percentage of everything we earn, no matter how much or how little, must be given to charity, he says. *It's the law in my country.*

I'm impressed. *That's really beautiful*, I say.

I think about the way Jews are supposed to give ten percent of their earnings to *Tzedakah*, or charity, too. I think about how few people I know actually do that. Making it the law seems like a really good policy.

We arrange to meet his friends at a buffet restaurant near where he lives at Yonge and Eglinton.

Malik's friends are nice. Most of them are from his city, or other cities in Saudi Arabia. One guy is from Jordan, and another is Palestinian but grew up in Egypt. He talks about the racism he's endured there—how there's no work for his father in the West Bank, how they went to Egypt with huge hopes, how life was so difficult for them there.

I want to say something, I have to. I tell them I have a good friend from back home who was from Israel. Malik laughs and strokes my hand.

Look what a nice girl she is, he says condescendingly, *trying to be friends with everyone. We're not allowed to go there, until it becomes a Palestinian state.*

I swallow hard.

The guy from Jordan tells me how, growing up, his geography teachers would tell him to cross Israel off the map because it didn't exist.

Another guy tells us proudly how he put an X through Israel on the map of the world in his ESL class. *It has all these maps on the bottom, one for each country, but I got rid of theirs.* He laughs.

Malik's reaction shocks me the most. *I got a lecture the other day at school about my views on Hitler,* he says. *I don't know why it pissed people off so much; all I said was that I didn't understand why people in Canada hated him so much. I mean, he helped us a lot—he rid the world of a lot of Jews. We like him in Saudi Arabia.* A couple of his friends nod.

I can't listen anymore. I can't believe how naïve I've been. It doesn't matter how open-minded or not religious I am. If these guys knew I was Israeli, they'd arrange to have me killed. I find myself getting up, grabbing my bag and jacket, walking out onto the street, ignoring them as they shout after me. Malik's getting up, coming after me. I jump into the first cab I see, turn the ringer off on my phone.

I don't know where else to go, so I go to work. I don't know if Lukas is home, and I don't want to have to explain myself. Marlize is serving, and Dez is making drinks behind the bar. I'm still shaking. I ask him to pour me some rum, some Jim Beam, some shots, shot after shot of strong stuff, as I swivel on my bar chair, trying to take it all in. Trying to figure out what I think, how to react.

It's Thursday, karaoke night. Some girl is singing that awful Paula Cole song, "Where Have All the Cowboys Gone," totally irony-free. It reminds me of elementary school, when the song came out. Running around on the playground at my school in Israel, playing soldiers with other kids. Things are simple as a kid: you love Israel and you hate the Arabs. Or at least you fear them. You believe soldiers are heroes, fighting for your right to live in your apartment, in your own country. When your dad says, *Push them all into the sea*, you agree with him.

This was before you get older and want to like them. Before you're dumb enough to hope for peace. Before you want to be their friend, or date them. Before they're real to you, a phantom enemy you occasionally see in the supermarket, or on the bus. Before they blow up buses your friends are on, and markets or pizza places.

Before the army, before basic training, before learning to fire a gun, before figuring out how pointless it all is. Before travelling, before meeting Muslims I loved in Morocco, in the UK, in Toronto. Before meeting a Saudi Arabian guy I wanted to be with.

Before my thoughts got more complicated than I could manage.

I scowl at Dez. *I thought this was a rock and roll bar. What the fuck is this shit?*

He smiles at me. *Then change it, baby. When she's done, sing something else. How about something by Black Flag?* I shrug, pick TV Party. At least it doesn't require actually being able to carry a tune.

He gives me a small glass of Scotch, and I gulp it down.

When I get up to our tiny stage, I ignore the lyrics as they flash on the blue screen in front of me.

I don't realize what I'm singing till I hear the words come out of my mouth.

Kol od balevav penima
Nefesh yehudi homiya
As long as deep in the heart
The soul of a Jew yearns ...

I'm singing Israel's nation anthem. I'm singing *Hatikvah*, which in English means "The Hope."

I don't stop til I'm done, singing it as loudly as I can over the dissonant guitars of an eighties punk band. A few people clap, probably thinking I'm singing world music or something. A few people looked stunned.

I scuttle back to the bar, try to make some jokes with Dez, try to laugh, not cry, as the floor starts spinning in circles. An hour or so later, I pass out, and one of them, probably Dez, drives me home.

We haven't talked about it since, and I hope we don't have to.

They probably think I'm crazy.

I'm starting to think I might really be going out of my mind.

Marlize

I got pregnant on a night that Dez came over late, about two weeks before I met his wife. It was the first week of May in Toronto, and everyone said it was unseasonably hot. It was only twenty-five degrees, but it was much more humid than Cape Town. I don't have air-conditioning. I'd been walking around in a pair of his boxer briefs, no bra. I'd tied my hair up in a ballet bun, which he'd always told me he loved. Little pools of sweat had gathered underneath my breasts, in my belly button, on the insides of my elbows.

You look so sexy, he said, *like you've been up all night just waiting for me.*

I actually have, I said, and laughed, feeling awkward in my obvious display of love.

He bit my neck and licked my nipples. He tore off my shorts, my fingers grabbed at the buttons on his jeans. He'd stopped to pick up some lube on the way, the kind that had the words *extra heat generating* on the bottle.

If you make me any hotter I'll die, I panted. We fucked on the bed, the hardwood bedroom floor, the cool grey marble of the passageway outside the bathroom. He went down on me twice with the glee of a kid in a candy store.

I can never get enough of you, he said. We did it standing up, sitting down, from behind, which hurt less than I expected, and doggy style.

Two hours later I was lying on his sweaty chest, brushing hair out of his eyes. He reached down absently, touched me down there softly, and pulled out a torn piece of latex. The condom had broken inside me. We'd been going so hard and so fast and it was so good that I hadn't felt it break.

I started to cry, and panic. I couldn't breathe. It was 3:00 a.m., and I had no idea where to find a twenty-four-hour pharmacy. The Shoppers near my apartment closed at 12:00.

I'd stopped taking the pill two weeks before. It'd had caused my skin to break out and my breasts to feel tender. It had made my mood swings worse than ever. The day before my period last month I cried so much I had to leave work early. I figured we were using condoms and that was enough. They're ninety-nine percent effective, or something like that. I knew how to use them, and he definitely knew how.

Is okay, baby, is okay, he said, pressed my body into his shoulder, my face into his neck. *It'll be okay, I'm sure it'll be fine. It happens. We'll wait a few days, take a test, but I'm sure you'll be fine.* He kissed my forehead. *It's happened to me before, a few years ago, she didn't get pregnant.* I looked up at him, looked into his eyes. I wanted to believe him so I did.

What happened, I asked, my throat still sounding like it was full of tears.

I was a lot younger, I was in Brazil, we were in high school. I felt a twinge of jealousy hearing this, and I hated myself for it.

I told the girl's mom, we were so freaked out, and she told us it would be okay. She told her to go take a piss, that it would get some of it out, you know? And it worked.

I looked at him in disbelief. *Are you serious? That's the stupidest thing I've ever heard. No one in the world would ever get pregnant, Dez.*

Leo, call me Leo, Marli, he said. *I like it better.*

I smiled.

I'll take you to get a test tomorrow, okay meu amour? *But I'm sure it'll be okay.*

He drove me to the drugstore down the street at 7:30 a.m., and sure enough, the test came back negative.

See? I told you, he said, kissing my neck. We bought more condoms too, more expensive ones, that kind with the words *extra durability* on them.

I took another test a few days later and it came back negative too, so I stopped worrying about it.

When I was late the next month I wasn't worried. I missed my period because I was stressed, I was busy, we were busy getting busy.

There was a lot going on. He'd finally told me he loved me and I was floating, daydreaming in class and dancing around at work, being open with everyone. I switched shifts with Nicki every time she asked. I started conversations with her, listened to her ramble about politics and Israel. I decided that she wasn't even that bad. We went shopping and saw a movie together, a girly romantic comedy that we both laughed at. I even gave a neighbour's little girl a hug when she came knocking at the door to sell us cookies.

I was happy all the time. I'd managed to do the impossible: have a really fun fling somehow turn into something meaningful. I loved him, and he said he loved me.

I let myself relax and believe it.

When the second month came with no period, I couldn't deny it anymore. I was either hungry all the time, or queasy. I was getting fat around the hips. My nipples felt so raw I couldn't ignore it.

And then I found out about his wife, and I didn't think I had a choice.

I go by myself to a hospital, and I take care of the whole thing without him.

He calls me today, but I ignore him. What would I say anyway? How can things ever be okay now?

I cry more now than I ever did before or during the abortion. I call my best friend Lanelle at 6:00 a.m. South African time, hysterical, wondering why this happened to me, what I can do to fix all of it, make everything like it was before, if that's possible. She listens.

I think about him all the time, I bawl. *I don't know what to do with myself now.*

Sterkte, she says, be strong.

Losing him has been harder for me than anything else in a long time.

Nicki

I didn't ever realize how much I miss home. I didn't allow it to occur to me.

You have to move forward, I tell myself over and over.

There's no time to dwell on these things.

I repeat it over and over to myself, like a mantra, until it becomes true.

Block it out until you believe it, until you've made enough of a success of your life to allow yourself to look back. Squash it, shove it down.

If I do think about home, I focus on the negatives, which, if I'm honest, is not that difficult to do.

It's hard to make a living in Israel. The politics are confusing and divisive. Your national ID number allows the government access to any and all information on you. It's overpopulated. In the summer it's oppressively humid. Everyone has to go to the army. Your job in the army is based on your high school grades, and the job you get after is based on your work ethic and success there.

Guess who gets sent to the trouble zones, to Gaza or Sderot or the West Bank, whether it's to be a fighter or a tank driver or an army data entry person? Not a straight-A student in grade twelve, that's for sure. Who gets the great high-paying jobs after? Not those guys either. It all accumulates, and by the time you're twenty-one or twenty-two it's all been figured out.

I'm twenty-four, and I've been to more funerals of people my age than weddings and bar mitzvahs combined. It's just a part of life there. You go to the funeral and cry, put stones on the grave, watch a young body get put gingerly into the ground, sometimes dropped in by hysterical parents who'd hoped their kid might outlive them. In Israel we don't use caskets, it's a religious thing, something about returning the body into the earth. I've been to thirty funerals now, friends, friends of friends, distant cousins, neighbours. I don't miss them at all.

There are hardly any pubs or bars at home, and alcohol is expensive. Dating involves an unusual amount of game-playing on the woman's part. I think it comes back to religion, being told 'no' from teachers and parents, learning to use sex as a weapon of power and control. No woman I know there seems to have sex for fun, unless she's in a long-term relationship or married, so she knows it's okay.

Before I left, I had a one-night stand with a guy called Or. I had to do it all—I made all the first moves, I kissed him first in the front seat of his car, supplied the condoms and we did it in his backseat, windows fogged up, feet pushing against the glass.

At mamash zoremet, he said to me, you really go with the flow. It sounds poetic in English but it was what Israeli guys said there when girls were slutty but they liked it anyway. It was embarrassing in hindsight. I had been flowing like a wave and hitting the sand softly, enjoying myself without any calculating or consequence. I'd left the next day so I didn't have to wait for a text from him that never came. I didn't have to sit around regretting it, feeling terrible, facing my girlfriends with their knowing looks.

In Israel people were always telling you what they thought, whether you asked them or not. People refused to stand in line, got into screaming fights with cashiers and waiters, constantly tried to rip each other off.

And yet, it was a place where people were warm, like me. Where people's hearts and minds were on their sleeves, where you never had to guess where you stood with anyone. People got angry fast, but got over it really quickly. When I thought about my city Ra'anana now, I was surprised to find my cheeks were wet, my mascara running. It was comfortable, and familiar, a place where I had history. I had memories from my teenage years and my childhood ricocheting in my head every time I thought of a street or a storefront.

I'd forgotten what that felt like. My whole life, it seemed like I'd dreamed about escaping, to anywhere, to what Israelis call *Khul*—an acronym for *Khutzlaretz*, any country outside of Israel.

I don't expect to feel so happy when my father offers to pay for me to fly home for a visit. I don't expect to feel so emotional at the thought.

I wonder what would happen if Lukas wanted to come with me. I wonder if he'd like it, if he'd see any of the beauty I see, if he'd love it too. I ask my father if they'd consider paying for Lukas too, if he could come with me.

We don't want to lose you, my father says, his voice catching at the back of his throat. *We don't approve—of him not being Jewish, or you two living together before marriage, of any of it, but we want to meet him. We want to see you.*

I can tell he's trying as hard as he can, and it's killing him.

I want Lukas to come with me to my city, to see it, to understand me more. I want him to experience everything with me. I want him to really see me.

Lukas

She comes home with round-trip tickets to Israel.

I look it up online and it says they cost at least three thousand dollars for the pair, possibly four.

She goes on and on about how special it's gonna be to go home with her.

She tells me her father paid for the tickets, her father who she doesn't get along with.

He really wants to meet you, she says.

The guilt's building up in my chest, rising like bile.

I can't, I want to tell her. *I can't, I can't, I can't.* But I say nothin'.

I listen to her jabber, on and on, about travellin' the length of her country, from north to south.

We can start in my town, go to Tel Aviv, Herzliya, the whole Sharon area, she's sayin'. *We can go to the beach, go shopping, I can take you all around. Then we can drive to the north, where there are all these amazing places, like Zimmer, where you're surrounded by nature—trees and grass and wild rabbits and it's just so beautiful. I want to show you Caesarea, and Zikhron Ya'akov, there's this artist area I love, and Haifa. The Bahá'í gardens there are really something to see. And we can end up in Eilat, this beach city, the country's southernmost point. It's cheesy because of the clubs and trance music, and the American tourists, but we can go snorkelling and scuba diving there. The fish are fluorescent—you can't believe they exist in real life, but they do. We're going to have the most amazing time there. You can meet all my friends.*

I have to stop her. I have to run outside, down the stairs of our building, past the lobby, into the small grassy patch of front yard. I have to throw up. Chunks rise in the back of my throat and I can't stop them. My eyes are watering. I wait until my body's completely emptied itself out before I turn around to go back. She hasn't followed me.

I can see that I'm finally gonna have to tell her the truth.

Dez

I fool around today with the girl who bartends across the street. I think her name is Stacey, but it could be Tracey. Anyway, she's been making eyes at me for weeks, and I registered it somewhere in the back of my head, but forgot.

I go over today and tell her how great she looks. *My girlfriend just broke up with me, and I'm lonely*, I say. That's all it takes.

We hardly say a word to each other. Just in and out, wham, bam, thank you ma'am.

I have to fake it for the first time in my life just to end it sooner.

I can't imagine actually talking to her, telling her anything about myself or actually listening to anything she has to say. I can't imagine caring about her.

🌍

Marlize was always telling me she loved me, long before I ever told her.

I know, she said, the night when I finally said it. *I've known for ages*, and it was one of those moments that was so perfect I wanted to take a picture, so I could always remember exactly the way everything looked and sounded. I took a picture with my phone of her bare back, her milky white skin, her bumpy spine, her slender hips, the backs of her ribs. You can see some of her hair in the shot, blonde and straight, the ends curling into little tendrils.

I loved kissing her neck. It was willowy and delicate, and her skin was soft.

🌍

I'm supposed to have an encounter tonight with one of the girls who works at the goth clothing store at Queen and Spadina.

Her name is Emily, and she likes being tied up. She's into what she calls light bondage. She wants to take me to a private fetish party at some guy's house. A bunch of strangers dressed in corsets and PVC doing all kinds of things to each other, while others watch them. For the first time in my life, I'm going to have to call a girl and turn her down. I think I'll text her, it'll be easier. I've never wanted to do anything less in my life.

Lukas

When Nicki and I first started dating, she loved goin' grocery shopping together. She found it fascinating to go to Loblaws. *It's so American*, she'd say, *the things you buy*.

Canadian, I'd correct her and she'd laugh. I knew she didn't understand or give a shit about the difference.

We'd each have our own baskets. In my basket would be the basics: Kraft dinner, Beefaroni, hot dogs, ketchup, Wonder Bread, hot dog buns, Heinz beans in tomato sauce, frozen pizzas with the works, frozen fries, pasta, and No Name brand pasta sauce. I'd never spent more than fifty bucks a week in my entire life.

Nicki's basket would be full of all things exotic and strange. She'd buy giant Fuji apples, wasabi peas, instant curry that reminded her of her time in India, vanilla soy milk, organic granola and yogurt, cedar plank salmon (which she pronounced *sall-mon*), cinnamon (which she pronounced *kin-a-mon*—the last part, *mon*, she'd say like a guy from Jamaica who I work with at the hospital says *man*. I'd try to correct her, but she'd just shrug and say that this was how they pronounced it in Israel), extra salty feta and goat's cheese (she could spend up to twenty minutes in the cheese aisle), eggs, tomatoes and cucumbers (to make the chopped salad she ate first thing in the morning every day for breakfast). She'd always spend well over a hundred, even a hundred and fifty bucks on herself and then she'd end up throwin' half of it out.

That was in the beginning when we still did stuff together. Back then Nicki was more accommodating. We'd watch TV and movies together, go for walks downtown, listen to music. We liked to do a lot of the same stuff: watch reruns on TV, get high and listen to the Beatles, talk about our lives when we were kids. After a while Nicki wanted to do her own thing, and we were both workin' more, so we spent more and more time apart. I'd see her, down the street from where we lived, sitting in a booth in McDonald's or Burger King, just fuckin' stuffing her face. I went in once, and watched her. She was sittin' in a corner, with a burger, two orders of fries, a chocolate shake, and a melting ice cream sundae. She was sweating as she ate, it was disgusting.

I hate myself, she cried, and I could see why. Her face was swollen and bloated, her eyes were red from cryin', her skin was broken out, her stomach ballooned with ripples of fat. She was covered in purple stretch marks across her hips. I felt like an asshole for thinkin' it, but I wasn't attracted to her anymore. We hardly ever had sex, and if we did, we both wanted the lights off. I was kinda disgusted every time I had to look at her in harsh, bright lighting.

We talked about it once—about tryin' to make it work, about what we could do to make each other happier. She said I needed to stop disappearing at night, that I needed to spend more time with her. I told her she had to fix her skin and lose some weight. She wasn't skinny when we first met, but I thought she was hot. I wanted to want her again.

I know no one will get it if I try to explain. They'll think I'm a piece of shit for judging her like that. But is it so wrong for a guy to look at his girlfriend and want to fuck her? It's not like I want a perfect ten, or even an eight or nine. I'd say at best, Nicki's probably a six and a half or a seven. I'm totally happy with that.

The problem with Nicki is that she needs me too much. I know she'll have problems findin' anyone else who wants her. I can't just dump her and that makes me even more pissed off.

I start workin' more hours and travellin' more just to get away from the rage I feel every time I have to talk to her.

Marlize

When he comes to see me, I'm lying in the same position on the couch, knees in, arms and head on the left arm. I'm exactly where I was two days ago when he called. I've only moved to go to the bathroom, get a drink of water, stay hydrated. It occurs to me that at some point, I may not feel like dying. Anything is possible. Remember to replace fluids.

My eyes are red-rimmed, puffy underneath. My cheeks are burning from too much salt.

Balled up tissues, toilet paper balls rolled up, are tucked into the crevices of the couch, lie in small piles at my feet. He sits on the floor, next to me, and I say what I've been thinking for hours, that if I had known I would have tried to understand.

Leo, I say, *I have to tell you something.* It takes a while, but I get it out. I tell him about the abortion. *That's why I haven't been talking to you*, I say. *It's not just because of her.*

He looks shocked. *I...I...I really didn't know*, he says. *I mean, we took a test. I thought everything was fine. I was trying to call you, all the time. I thought you weren't at work because you wanted to avoid me. You wouldn't talk to me. I really didn't know.*

I nod. *I know. I know. Of course you didn't know.*

What I say next is really hard but I know I have to say it. *Leo, I don't know if I can still see you knowing that you're married. I don't think I can. I mean, I want to understand this whole situation but . . .*

He hesitates before he answers me, and when he does, he is matter-of-fact. *Marlize*, he says, *no offence, but this situation is so complicated that I'm not sure your understanding even enters into it.*

His tone is so cold that I actually feel chilly. I pull the fleece blanket up higher on me, send a pile of tissues cascading onto the floor next to him.

I don't know what to do about her. I really don't, he adds.

My mistake, I say, staring at the wall.

Look, I'm sorry this has been so messy, he says, using his hands to move in between us, this thing between us. *I never wanted it to be like this*, he says, in the same tone that he uses with pissed-off customers, trying to show that he's listening, and being sincere, when he's really laughing behind their backs.

I never thought he'd use that bullshit on me. I feel very sorry for him and really furious at the same time.

It is what it is, I spit out. *If you think it's over, then it must be.*

There's no use, I realize, fighting for something he doesn't really want. It's always the way he wants it, when he wants it.

His eyes are wide. *So that's just it then, we're never going to see each other, or talk again? That's the end, clean and easy?*

I blow my nose, push my thumbs into the corners of my eyes to keep the tears inside.

No. Yes. Maybe. I don't know, what do you want?

He gets up, moves to the arm of the couch, sits down on it, next to me. He smoothes some of the hair out of my face, and it feels nice. He runs his thumb over my cheeks and I close my eyes.

I don't know, he says, and closes his eyes too. *I really don't know.*

We sit like this for at least half an hour, not saying a word.

Before he leaves, he leads me to my bedroom, helps me into bed, pulls the sheet up on my face, underneath my nose, the way I like it when I want to fall asleep. He remembers small details, the kind that prick at the heart and leave me dazed for a second, but never the big things, never the things that really matter.

I'll come back and visit you soon, skat, he says, shuts the door softly behind him. I can't decide if I need him or I need to get my locks changed, if I want him in or out of my life forever. I love him more and in a different way than I have ever loved anyone.

I wonder why no one tells you what to do with yourself when loving someone isn't enough.

Lukas

She comes home complaining about her body. She's eaten too much at work she says, crunchy nachos with gooey, bubbling yellow cheese, salsa and sour cream, hot dogs, burgers, buffalo wings, cupcakes, beer, rum and cokes.

She doesn't ask me how I am, or where I've been. We've gotten past that point. She doesn't try to tell me what happened to her that day, or the day before. She just walks by me, topless, covering her pepperoni-sized nipples with her palms, elbowing the purple stretch marks creeping up her belly. She claws at her stomach bulges like she wants to rip her own skin off, her tits flapping, pulled down to her bellybutton by gravity.

I'd just spent the night cleaning an area full of terminally ill patients.

I was only freaked out by one girl, a nineteen-year-old who'd been there for seven months.

Her name was Mandy. She had a corner room, with a mini-fridge stocked with food.

Her walls were covered, floor to ceiling, with cut-outs of celebrities.

She wore grey-striped pyjama bottoms and a pink flowered t-shirt. She had an intravenous drip connected to her face to make sure she ate, but the nurses said she was always in trouble for ripping it out.

She walked around barefoot, her bones poking out of her ankles and toes.

I was cleaning her room when a youth worker, around my age or younger, came in to work with her. The youth worker was this over-the-top cheery woman, and Mandy was not havin' it.

Let's paint, the youth worker said, and set up the colours. Mandy kicked 'em to the floor. *How are you feeling right now,* she asked her, speaking slowly and loudly.

I'm fucking sick of this place, Mandy screamed. *Why don't you people just let me die?*

The youth worker left in tears and Mandy sat on her bed, triumphant.

I don't know what came over me, I don't usually talk to patients. *What the fuck is wrong with you,* I snapped. *There's a guy down the hall with flesh-eating disease, the old lady next door has bronchial disease and is waitin' for a new lung, there's another guy who's ninety-eight, and a cold could kill him, and you, you're doin' this to yourself? The cure is food, and there's lots of food in your fridge, and in this fucking city, you don't have to do this.* I was shakin'.

She looked at me, her eyes swimming with tears. *I don't know why,* she said. *Do you like yourself?* she asked me.

I didn't know how to answer that honestly. *No,* I found myself sayin'. *Not at all.*

This is my way of punishing myself for all the bad things I've done, she said.

I went back to my cleaning.

✹

Nicki's sittin' on our bed, naked, poking at herself. She's cryin'. *I hate my body,* she's sayin', and in that moment, I don't feel love or even pity for her.

Lukas, you never make me feel good anymore, she says. *You never make me feel beautiful, you never make me feel loved. . . .*

I don't know what's happenin' until my skin makes contact with her face, until I realize I've hit her again, til I hear her screamin' at the top of her lungs.

She runs into the bathroom, and locks the door, stays inside for close to an hour.

When she comes out, she's curiously calm.

I'm moving out, she said. *I don't ever want to see you again.*

I try to apologize, it seems like the right thing to do, but she won't let me.

She packs up all her stuff in less than hour.

Where the fuck are you goin', I ask her, but she won't tell me. I run after her, down the street, but she runs faster. When I call CDRR later, none of them will tell me where she is.

I keep callin' back until one of the kitchen staff tells me to stop. He says they've been told to call the cops.

I haven't heard from her in two weeks, and I have no idea where she is.

I know that we don't have much left, but a part of me hopes that we still have something.

Marlize

Last night I dream we have a daughter.

Her face is palm-sized, her amber hair crackles with red heat, her skin is soft and translucent.

She can fit into doll's clothing, our living doll, she can wear the navy blue- and green-checked sailor dress that belongs to a Madame Alexander doll I had as a kid. Her limbs are thin and fragile, her elbows knobby. I sit her on a chair, in between my twin plastic dolls, their eyes beady, hers looking soft like Dez's. She has his focused stare, the slight smile around the corner of his lips. She's radiant. She looks at me and my heart cracks. I can't believe she's mine, ours.

Let's give her a real English name, I say to Dez, *like Elizabeth or Diana. I want her to feel like a queen or princess.*

Elizabeth is perfect, he says, *my sister's name is Liz.* He's happy. He kisses her and then me on the top of my head and goes off to the bar to work. I'm by myself. She's sitting there, playing with one of the dolls.

I turn around for a second, stare out the window, watch a cardinal hop from one branch to another on a tree. I hear a crash, turn back and see her hit the floor, lunging for her but it's not fast enough. Her face hits the marble and cracks like porcelain into tiny, sharp slivers. I have to help her, she doesn't make a sound, not a sound, I have to tell Dez, I have to clean up the mess, I'm so confused. I pick up the pieces, her dress, crying, drive us to the hospital.

The doctor tells me that I've done it on purpose, that I didn't love her, didn't appreciate her enough. As punishment he cuts open my uterus, wants to examine it up close, figure out what's wrong with me. Clouds of dust pour out of me, fill the room til I'm coughing, choking.

Your body is like a kiln, he tells me, *firing up bits of dust and water, instead of flesh and blood. Elizabeth was made of clay and bones. She was fragile, and she died. You couldn't take care of her. You can't have children, Marlize. Your body is wrecked. You're not human.*

I feel myself sweating, water pouring down my temples to the sides of my face. I'm about to have a panic attack, to run screaming out of the room, when I wake up with a jolt.

I feel my forehead, and my face, but it's bone dry.

I go to the kitchen, fumble in the dark for my cigarettes, a bottle of red wine. I also grab what's left of the Nutella, and a spoon. I turn on the TV. It's 2:36 a.m. I know I can't go back to sleep now. I wouldn't dare to try to.

At 6:00 a.m. I'm lying on my back, on the couch. I try to sleep. I close my eyes, think of comforting things.

I think of swimming in my parents' pool as a kid. I think of my sister, of my dog. I think of my mom.

I sing to myself, that song from Mary Poppins that she sings to the kids to get them to fall asleep. It always worked for me when I was little, to sing it to myself that "Stay Awake" song. It's all about reverse psychology—in an incredibly soothing voice, she encourages them not to try to sleep, and they drift off halfway through. It used to work on me too.

When I finally drift off, I dream about another baby, about having a fat baby boy. A boy who loves to laugh and eat and sleep. He's perfect and healthy. We adore him. Dez buys him a green, blue, yellow and white onesie: the colours of Brazil's soccer team.

He's going to be a football player, he says, *got to get him into it now.* He buys him a plush black and white mini-ball to play with, gently passes it to him.

He's so loving, so devoted, he makes my heart melt. One day we're standing in the kitchen, the baby's face smeared with mashed banana, and Dez hands the baby to me, says it's my turn to change his diaper.

I take him gently, hold him by the waist, but he tries to get away from me. It doesn't feel natural, I have to put him down. He wriggles and I forget, forget to support his head, and I slide on the wet tiles and I drop him. He hits the floor, head first, his skull dented, screaming, he's screaming so loudly. Dez lets out a cry that could've come out of a wounded animal, and

I wake up before he can tell me what damage I've done. Before anyone has a chance to tell me that I've ruined everything.

That I'll never be a parent. That I'm a monster.

I've let Dez down. That's what hurts most, more than anything.

I've broken his heart by not telling him. I have no idea how to protect him.

I have no idea how to love the person I thought I loved the most.

I have no idea what to do with the guilt I'm feeling.

Dez

My crotch is on fire. I wake up to find myself scratching so hard that I'm bleeding.

I stand in the shower, hungover, dousing myself with soap and body wash, trying to figure out what's happening. I even trim my pubes so I can get a closer look. Tiny dots are moving in the hairs under my shaft. I get dressed and run to the closest walk-in clinic at Queen and Spadina. It's dingy, with a graffiti-tagged sign out front, and piles of papers and patient files everywhere.

The doctor establishes right away that I have an STD. She asks me questions about how many partners I've had, if I'm single, if I know who could've given it to me. I shake my head. *More than a hundred, yes, I really don't know.*

I did end up going to that party, having sex with four of the girls there, and getting a blow job from the girl who invited me, Emily. I think about that bartender, who texted me about seeing me again, and momentarily, about Marlize.

I take off my pants, and the doctor combs through my hair using a white light.

Mr. Da Silva, you have pubic lice, or what people commonly refer to as crabs. You need to use Pediculicide, a special shampoo, on it twice a day for the next four days. You need to make sure you put on clean underwear and pants after each treatment, and wash everything, including your sheets, on the hot cycle of your washing machine.

As I get up to leave, I wonder what Marlize would say, how embarrassed she would be, how angry and upset with me. I wonder what Adriana would say. I can hardly believe it myself. All these years of living like this, and this is my first STD. I decide to get tested for everything else. It will be three days before I get my HIV result. I know I won't be able to sleep if I think about it.

Oh, and Mr. Da Silva, the doctor adds, walking me to the waiting room, in front of two girls and a guy, who are sitting on the cracked leather seats. *Don't engage in any sexual activity for at least a week. And please, make sure you always use condoms.*

I guess I have it coming for being the world's biggest, most irresponsible asshole.

Dez

I sit down on the living room floor. The carpet's burning my calves, rubbing against my thighs.

I'm wearing shorts. Adriana's dressed up, dressed to devastate me in a tight black dress and red lipstick. Clouds of Stella McCartney perfume surround her. I know, because I used to have to buy it for her all the time. She'd hint and cough and point it out when we saw it, then act surprised when I dropped $150 dollars on her.

She sits on the couch. We talk shit for a while, the weather, the news, her family. I tell her she looks good.

Leo, she says abruptly, Tan na hora. *It's time. We need to get a divorce. I've met someone.*

What? When?

About a year ago, she says. *He asked me to move in with him last month. He wants to put my name on his lease, but he won't, until I get all this*—she gestured wildly around her—*organized.*

A year ago, I explode. *A year ago. You were waiting here the other day*, voce acabou com todo, *you ruined everything, over something that had already happened ages ago, when you could've waited for a better time. And you knew it, you just didn't care. You know what? Maybe I don't want a divorce anymore. I don't need to be single now. I don't care.*

You can't be serious about that girl, that tall skinny little girl—she spits the words out with disgust—*the girl with the stupid, bowled-over look on her face, the girl who didn't even know who I was, who didn't even know you were married.*

She stops for a minute. She's studying my face.

O, meu Deus, she says, *oh my God. You are. You're serious about her.* Voce esta apaixonado por ela. *You're in love with her.*

Sí, I say, looking away from her. *Yeah, I think I am.*

Did you ever love me, she asks me, staring at the wall.

I rub my temples with my fingers, make smooth circles on my skin before I answer her.

I don't know. We were young. I don't know. Did you love me?

Yes, she says, without any hesitation.

I'm shocked when the tears come, when they pour out of my eyes for what feels like hours.

I sit there, shaking, holding my legs with one arm to steady me, holding my face with my other hand.

The last time I cried was at my father's funeral.

I'm sorry, I say, *I'm so sorry.*

She puts her arm around me. *Eu sei,* she says, I know.

She gets up to make some coffee.

What are we going to do, I ask her, *about the house, about the club?*

You'll sell the house, she says, *and we'll split the profits. We'll make a plan about the club. I don't know yet. But you love it, I know. We'll keep it running somehow.*

What am I going to do about my mother, I ask. *This will kill her.*

Let me talk to her, she says. *Let me call her first.*

I give her a hug on her way out. *Obrigada por tudo,* I say, thank you for everything.

My eyes are still blurry. Adriana holds me for what felt like days. *You deserve to be happy, Leo,* she says.

Tudo o mundo merece ser feliz. Everyone in the world deserves their own happiness.

I write a letter to my mom that night.

In it I write that I'm sorry for everything—for going against everything she's ever taught me, for never living my life the way I was supposed to.

I tell her the truth—that I don't know why. Is it a lack of self-control? Bad judgement?

Why am I inclined towards things that people like my sisters and classmates and friends naturally know to avoid? I really don't know.

It isn't the kind of person I want to be.

I want to be a good person, I write. *I want to learn to navigate between my desires and the right thing to do. I want to enjoy my life without hurting people. I feel terrible for hurting Adriana, and hurting you.*

You have to believe me—it's not a mistake for us to get divorced—it was a mistake for us to get married.

I've met a new girl that I think I love—yes mom, I think I'm in love. I can't believe it either.

I want to be with her. I want to try to be good enough for her. I don't know if I can do it, but I want to try. I have to try. But I can only try if you forgive me. Can you forgive me, mom? Will you ever forgive me? I live in hope.

I can't decide whether I want to mail it or burn it, so for hours I do nothing.

Adriana calls me the next afternoon. I'm asleep on the couch and the ringer on the phone is so loud I actually jump.

She gets straight to it, like always. Not even time to ask me how I am, whether I slept at all.

It's moments like this, I think, *where I know I'm making the right decision.*

Your mom was devastated, of course, Adriana says, *but not as shocked as we expected. We talked for a long time. She misses you. I think everything will be okay. You have to call her though.*

I sigh. *I will*, I say. *Tomorrow, or the next day. I still need time.*

Next year your mom says she'll come visit you, Adriana says. *If you and the kid get married.*

I sigh again. *I have no idea if Marli will even take me back.*

I have to down half a bottle of scotch and do four of lines of coke before I finally have the guts to call her.

Nicki

In the time that I was with Lukas, I gained thirty-five pounds. Enough to effectively make me invisible to men, and enough to make me the subject of scorn and snickering, dirty looks and palpable pity from other women. I knew it was happening, but I couldn't stop myself. Every time he ignored me, every time he hid things from me, every time I had feelings that I didn't know what to do with, that I couldn't acknowledge to him because I knew how pointless it would be, I would shove food down.

At first it was fine; fun, indulgent even. I still felt like I was in control, ordering deep-dish pizzas with Canadian bacon, mushrooms and pineapple, pans of brownies, cheesecake or Oreo ice cream, fried chicken, French fries. I'd lie on the couch in my underwear and a tank top, high on carbohydrates. There's something infinitely comforting about having junk food delivered to your door, knowing that you could survive without ever having to leave the house.

Lukas was never around, always working weird hours or just disappearing without telling me where he was, so I never had to explain myself. I'd clean it all up, shove the evidence into garbage bags and take it outside to our building's dumpster before he could notice it.

After a while I stopped being able to look at myself in the mirror. I had to cover all the mirrors in the house with towels so I wouldn't be tempted to look, like the Orthodox Jews do when they sit *shiva*. In a way, I was mourning. I was mourning a time when I felt like I was in control of my life. I was mourning the person I no longer hoped I could be.

The bulges on my sides disgusted me, the way I couldn't feel my ribs anymore, the way my stomach swelled and hung like a kangaroo's pouch. I didn't recognize myself, the way my inner thighs rubbed and broke into a rash in the heat, the cottage cheese cellulite on my thighs and ass.

When I first met Lukas, I was average by Israeli standards: not skinny, not fat, but closer to thin if I had to choose one. I'd had the run with dysentery in India that had left me lying on the bathroom tiles of my hostel for a week and a half, throwing up and going to the toilet every ten minutes. I lost about fifteen pounds. For a while after I got back to Israel, my hip bones stuck out. Everyone told me how fantastic I looked, despite the fact that I could've died. I suppose in a country where the summer lasts most of the year, looking good in a bikini is most people's priority. My weight had always fluctuated but I'd never been obese or anything, just chubby at times.

I didn't realize how bad it was until I found myself literally bursting out of my clothes—buttons popping off blouses, zippers breaking on skirts. I had to go shopping every month or so because nothing fit me. I stopped looking at sizes because it depressed me. I'd shop vintage, head to Kensington Market and buy dresses whose labels had long since fallen off, so I didn't have to think about what size I was wearing. A few people asked if I was pregnant. Our neighbours, this couple in their forties with two kids, stopped me to congratulate me one day, to tell me how happy they were for me and Luke.

You kids'll be very happy together, they said. I felt like I was going to be sick, but I went along with it because I wanted them to think that we were happy.

The wife pulled my short green jacket down over my stomach one slightly breezy night. *You don't want the baby to get cold*, she said. I wanted to punch her.

At the bar, I went from being a waitress men flirted with and tipped well to a waitress they mostly ignored, except to bark at when orders were wrong, or the wait was too long. In Israel, you could be a woman of fifty and you could expect to be hit on in the convenience store, in the supermarket, at the gas station. Your body type and looks were irrelevant. I didn't think I'd ever miss that, but I do. There's something about it that makes you feel eternally attractive and womanly no matter what.

A part of me never really believed that Lukas loved me, as much as I wanted to believe it. Every pound I gained was a test that he failed, I saw it in his eyes, the contempt, the disgust, and in the last few months I heard it in his tone, in his lack of affection, in his words. He'd stopped caring about me as a person. To me, the body had always seemed like a superficial thing—the carrier for what was important: the mind, the heart, the spirit. I'd been attracted to all kinds of guys in my life: beefy and slight, lanky and short. I'd liked all eye colours, all hairstyles, all kinds of dressers, from guys with ironed cotton shirts and dress pants to shorts and sandals. It just never meant that much to me. I'd always wanted to be open to everything.

Lukas started gaining weight by the end too. His pants got too tight around his thighs and ass, he went up a size in shirts, got round around his chin, but it didn't change my feelings for him. How could he judge me in a way that I'd never judge him? The injustice of it made me furious.

I felt powerless. I couldn't stop myself from eating tens of thousands of calories a day. I couldn't understand what we were doing together anymore and I felt trapped, but I was afraid to leave. I still loved him, and a part of me desperately still wanted to make it work. I had committed myself. I'd gotten used to it. I asked him to come with me to Israel even after he hit me. I couldn't control myself from trying to mute the terrible feelings of inadequacy I had every time I spoke to him. I didn't know how I would ever recover the confidence I'd once had.

When I finally left him, I found that I felt less hungry. After a month or so, it was just weight again, just numbers on a scale that I could manipulate if I changed my diet or exercised. I started eating less, and jogging and I started to look like me, but I still didn't feel the way I'd hoped I would. It was just my body, just the shell. Inside I was still incapacitated.

Dez

The truth about marriage is that no one ever goes into it thinking they're going to fail. You know it's a possibility, but you never really think it'll happen to you.

I don't believe that anyone is really okay with the thought that all that time, energy and love can leave you with nothing. I've lost a relationship, I've lost a kind of security, I've lost money and possessions, the ownership of my house and business.

I've lost face to my friends and family back home.

One day I'll have to go home and visit relatives who will have kept my wedding photos on display, because it was such a happy day for all of them. I'll have to justify myself over and over when the truth is that I still don't have an answer.

It wasn't really done in my parents' day to get a divorce.

Not in Brazil, my mother would say, *not in our church*.

I grew up with a dad who had a weekend apartment, mistresses that we met and whores that he bragged about as I got older, and a mom who was excessively religious. I never understood how or why it worked, but still I always thought that my parents must have been in love at one point.

I imagined it sometimes. My father, this handsome, swarthy man, meeting my mother, then young, not overweight and saddled with pain, fresh, unburdened, open and beautiful. Maybe they met across a crowded room. Maybe my dad used a pick-up line that was cheesy, and she laughed. Maybe he didn't know how to pick up chicks then, and he said something that came straight from his heart or brain or cock, but it was genuine and she was flattered. Maybe they flirted for a while, then started dating. Maybe he asked my grandfather's permission to take her out on dates, and then to marry her. Maybe my grandparents on both sides had been overjoyed, and their wedding was the most perfect day in history.

How could they have seen it coming, the differences of beliefs, the financial and emotional and physical needs that never went away no matter how many years they spent together?

How could they have known what they were signing up for?

I don't see how they could have lived with what they did to each other—his fucking around, her screaming and criticizing. How could they have stood being so unhappy for so long? How did they think their kids would turn out?

Even today, when it *was* done, when forty percent of marriages ended that way, it was still a shock to everyone, especially me, and I didn't think it was any less painful.

Marriage was such an undertaking—the asking, the wedding itself, the honeymoon, wearing the rings, using the words *my wife* all the time. A part of me must have thought that I would be with Adriana forever—in whatever dysfunctional way. It was how I was raised.

I really thought that in some way, it was normal. Or deep down, even if I knew it wasn't, I thought it was common enough. I thought that a lot of people lived in strange arrangements, for all kinds of reasons. I thought I could live like that for an overall appearance of being a family man with a joint business and success and a house and a life together. For the same dream that everyone seems to have everywhere, for the illusion of success.

It's how Marli was raised too, with her parents pretending to be happy while they secretly cheated on each other. She told me about it once, how she had kind of known but pretended that she hadn't because it had been too hard for her to acknowledge. She'd had her dancing to distract her until the attack, and then she came here and met me. When we started talking, I mean really sharing stuff, she suddenly had to think about it. We both had to face things that made us feel uncomfortable, things we hadn't been strong enough to deal with alone.

What are we doing, I sometimes wonder. Will we ever be able to give each other what we need? Will it end like my marriage, with my mother sobbing on the phone, with me feeling like I've lost everything I ever had?

I want to give it a try if she'll let me.

I want to love her.

I want our bad experiences—my mistakes and her trauma and our parents' fuck-ups—to cancel each other out. I think we're the perfect amount of damaged to balance each other out. I want us to be the cure for each other's disorders.

I want to be the little thing that makes her smile when she's in the middle of having a terrible day.

Nicki

I didn't leave him because it hurt, because I was scared he'd do it again, or because I couldn't defend myself against him.

I didn't do it because of the anger that twisted his features, that burned in his retinas, that shot out of his mouth, that bent his fingers into a fist when he punched my face.

I didn't leave him because in that moment he didn't seem human, or because in that moment or the ones leading up to it, he was deaf to anything I said, snarling, jumping down my throat.

I didn't fight back, because I *wanted* him to hurt me. I wanted it to be over.

That was the easy part, does that make sense?

I wanted him to hurt me, to do his worst, so that we were both sure it was over. Because for the past few weeks, that's what I'd known without a shadow of a doubt.

I didn't love him anymore. I wasn't sure I ever had.

I was just waiting, waiting for the right time to get out.

Waiting for the right moment to re-evaluate my life. Trying to figure out what my next move should be.

It wasn't a question of if, but when. Does that sound cold? I know I cared about him, of course. But I'd been slowly detaching for weeks, slowly getting my life back. I knew what he was capable of. He'd hit me before, and I'd tried, tried so hard to say it was okay, to understand it.

For the first time in a long time the future looks too wide open, too full of possibility.

I don't know what to do with myself so for a month I do nothing.

I move into a backpackers' hostel at Spadina and King to get away from him. I don't have a lot of stuff—just clothes and CDs, a few books, my camera, canvases, art supplies. I never had any furniture.

I take melatonin at night to help me fall asleep. I love that you don't need a prescription for it here the way you do in Israel.

I use an internet café nearby to contact friends. I go to work, but I change my shift hours so he can't find me. I go for walks by myself, or sometimes with Marlize. If we get off work at a decent hour, we take the streetcar east on Queen and go for walks on Woodbine Beach.

We make jokes about it—about the water you can't actually swim in, the lack of waves, the *E. coli*, the tons of sand the bulldozers must have brought in to make it look like a real beach.

It is pretty. We take our shoes off, sink our feet into the sand, listen to the water softly hit the rocks next to us. We point out familiar things: seagulls and volleyball nets and towels. We close our eyes and pretend we can smell the sea.

What's the beach like in Tel Aviv, compared to here, she asks me one day.

Well, the sand is dirtier than here, I say, and we both laugh. *In the summer the water can be as warm as a bath. It's always full of people, Israelis and tourists. Everyone's always having a good time. People drink at the beach—I used to love cold watermelon with vodka in it. It was like a big, boozy Slushie: perfect when it was boiling hot and humid. Israelis just know how to have fun. Couples make out all over the place. People leave work early just to take their kids to the beach sometimes. They do normal things, they jog or they walk their dogs but you can see that they're happy. They're not reserved like the people here. They don't have that guilt of "I'm taking time off," you know? They just do it.*

She nods. *Ja, South Africans have fun too. They also just know how.*

What was your favourite beach? I ask her. *In Cape Town.*

She closes her eyes. *Camp's Bay*, she says. *It's so beautiful, and it has this chilled out, holiday vibe. The water is deep blue, and warm, and the waves can be quite big. The sand is white. On the other side you can see the Lion's Head Mountains. They're so green and perfect in a way that almost isn't real, you know? I never realized how spoiled I was for beautiful views when I lived there.*

I nod. *I know what you mean.*

I take out some cheap red wine and she complains about how terrible it is, but still drinks it. It stains her mouth and makes her look like she's wearing lipstick from the nineties.

Sometimes I talk about Lukas and Marlize talks a lot about Dez. She says that they're thinking of getting back together.

Do you trust him? I ask her.

She looks down at her hands. *I think I probably have to*, she says.

No, but I mean, in your heart, do you believe he'll never cheat on you?

Her eyes are focused on the water. *I don't know.* She looks at me. *Do you remember what he was like when I first started working there? All those girls?*

Of course, I say. *I think everyone knew. I even warned you to stay away from him, remember? I waited on girls who came to the bar just to start with him. Sometimes they were really young, like eighteen or nineteen.*

She nods. *I think around the time that we got more serious.*

I noticed, I say. I really did. *But I didn't really put it together until I walked in on you guys that day.*

She smiles. *We were trying to be discreet. Oh, God. That was embarrassing.*

Was I the only one who ever saw you guys?

Ja, but others came close. Kitchen staff especially. Once José had a shift that started two hours earlier and Dez forgot. We were in a similar position except I was wearing a skirt and Dez was on his knees. I was panicking because I couldn't find my underwear and I didn't want him to stop because it was so great but we were so afraid of getting caught.

She pauses. *The adrenaline was so amazing. I had no idea sex could be that good.*

Did you guys ever—

She laughs. *Only if it was very late, like two or three in the morning and no one else was there.*

I try not to stare. *On the counter? The counter I pick up plates from?*

She giggles. *Don't worry, we cleaned it. But more often on the floor right next to it. The granite is cold.*

What's the best sex you've ever had, she asks me.

I think of Alon. *On a beach in Israel,* I say.

Really? What happened with the guy?

We broke up. We loved each other but I was never sure if we wanted the same things. I miss him sometimes.

She reaches over and touches my arm. I'm so startled I almost push her off.

I look at her. *How do you know that getting back together with Dez is actually the right thing to do?*

Marlize sighs. *I have no idea if it is. It's just something I have to do. It's not rational. I went through this terrible thing and I was so afraid of men. For some reason, I always trusted him. Even when we first met, I could talk to him in a way I couldn't talk to anyone else. In South Africa, I had a boyfriend who was always annoyed because he said I was on my own trip. I think Dez actually likes that about me. He doesn't expect me to be more emotional. When he says he loves me, I actually believe it. Do you know what I mean?* she asks me.

I nod slowly. *I actually do,* I say. *But what if he does cheat? He's a smart guy. He reminds me of a lot of guys I knew in Israel. He might just know how to hide it.*

Her eyes look watery. *It's true. It's hard to know. He could be an asshole. The problem is, I love him, Nicki—I think I have to try.*

Her hands are shaking. *My sister used to say that a person could only know whether or not they'd survive jumping off a cliff by actually jumping. And maybe it won't work out with Dez, but I've been through so much worse, and I didn't die then. At least I won't have any regrets.*

I smile. *That's an interesting way to think about it.*

Nicki, she says. *You were in the army. What's the worst that could happen to you if you got back together with this guy?*

I think about it. *I could be incredibly disappointed if it didn't work out again.*

Okay, but you'd get over it. It couldn't be worse than what happened with Lukas.

That's true, I say. *Alon's not that kind of guy, anyway. I can't imagine him being violent.*

You know Leo always hated Lukas.

Leo?

Dez's real name. He wouldn't tell me why, he just always called him a thug. I didn't like him either.

I'm touched that they thought so much about me. I didn't expect that at all.

We get up and start walking to the streetcar. *I don't know about you,* Marlize says, *but I'm finished living my life in fear of possible danger. It paralyzes you and stops you from living.*

When I get home that night I use the internet café to email Alon.

I don't have a subject line, and just write one line in the body. *Ani mitgaga'at eilecha.* I write, I miss you. He writes back two hours later, just one line.

Gam ani, it says. Me too.

Lukas

Something about it just feels inevitable. I'm Lukas and I hit people. I beat people up when they cross me. I'm an asshole, so sue me.

I always knew she couldn't deal with me. I always knew when she found out the truth about my past, how foolish I'd been, she'd go runnin' back to wherever she came from.

I knew I shouldn't have hit her but I kinda always knew that one day I'd snap. She grated at me til I just couldn't deal with her anymore.

It's not that I didn't love her. In my own way, I think I did, just like in her own way, I think that she might've loved me. But I've never known a love that lasts. I've never known a love that keeps goin', despite the obstacles. I've never been able to tell a girl about my past and have her accept me. No one has sympathy for you if you're a guy who's six-foot-four, and you tell them you hit a girl more than once. They treat you like you're poison.

Before we broke up, Nicki told me about how Dez had actually fallen in love with that Marlize girl, but he lost her because of his greasy womanizing ways. I saw it comin' and I wasn't surprised at all. She felt all sorry for him, you could tell. It made me furious because it made no sense.

Everyone has sympathy for people when they lose control with sex or drugs—no matter how disgusting or outta control they were. Why the fuck was it not like that with violence? What was the difference? All our problems were the same, when you thought about it, but people were afraid of me. They'd just see a monster with thousands of fists.

Nicki called the cops on me, but I hid in the alley near the dumpster out back, and they couldn't find me. I wasn't ready to be locked up again.

When I stopped to think about it, my chest felt like it was being smothered by boiling hot towels. Like I could just go up in flames any second.

When I looked back at school on the army bases, those times in my life I hated so much, now I thought, *At least the rules were clear.*

I had the easiness of knowing how to be good.

I had the feeling of bein' able to live with myself knowing I'd done everything I was supposed to do every day. I could sleep knowing it'd all been checked off a check list.

I thought I wanted to call my mom. I wanted to see how she was, ask her if I could live with her in Moncton. When I was younger, I kinda had fantasies of bein' in the navy.

A teacher I had on one of the military bases, who was also a military officer, once said that if I didn't come back to my roots, I'd only have done half a circle. He figured I'd spend the rest of my life tryin' to complete it. I really wanted him to be wrong—*I'm a fuckin' individual,* I said at the time. *I'm not a fuckin' cog in a machine, a sixteen-year-old on an assembly line, goin' to come out the other side as a real man.*

I wanted to live an interesting life. I wanted to travel and know the country like the back of my hand.

I wanted to live in Toronto because I had this fantasy of being anonymous and sophisticated. I liked that I could take the subway and hear at least five different languages at a time. I wanted to have a job, any job, eat fish and chips at this place I loved across from Trinity Bellwoods, stare out the window and make funny observations about people, like those guys in sitcoms set in cities like New York. I wanted to be anyone but the guy from the sticks with a past that everyone judged. I wanted to be with a girl from any other country, who'd seen and done more than me and would never pick up on the signs of who I really was. I wanted to be a good guy, and I wanted Nicki to be that girl, and I think she tried, but we were both unhappy. The real me was always gonna let her down. I was like a bad actor in a quality movie that I didn't deserve to be cast in.

I can't stay here now. I have to call my mom and beg her to let me live with her, get her to get me into some army training so that one day I can enlist. She's an army widow, for fuck's sake.

I think this could be rock bottom but I don't actually know. I can always sink lower. The thought of going back to my tiny town is not an option.

I hope begging will be enough.

I have nowheres else to go if she says no.

Dez

Being with Adriana by the end was like having a slab of concrete tied to my ankles. She had checked out emotionally—but it calmed me down in some way to know that she was there, even if just physically. My biggest fear was being alone, in a room or an apartment, anywhere really, to be stuck in my own company for too long with only my own thoughts to keep me occupied. Having someone else there—anybody really, it could even have been my mother—knowing that I wasn't going to sleep alone, or die alone in my apartment, or walk around talking out loud to myself—was all I needed.

The problem with Marli was that as much as I knew I loved her, I didn't have that history with her. I hated taking risks.

Even when we weren't living together anymore, knowing that I could call Adriana at any hour of the night—to have sex, to talk, talk about business, talk about Toronto, Brazil, anything—she would come, she would show up any hour of the night just because I asked her to. She'd show up just because I needed her—to watch a movie, even the ones I loved that she hated watching, old TNT movies like *Splendor in the Grass*, or *East of Eden*, anything with Natalie Wood or James Dean, to listen to underground music that she probably hated—and she'd be there because we were technically married and it was expected of her.

I tried to explain it to Marli once, recently, but she dissolved into tears.

The reason, I tried to explain, *that the divorce is so difficult is that Adriana is a known quantity*. I had known for a fact that she wanted to be with me for the rest of her life.

Marli was young, how could she make that kind of commitment? How could I ask her or expect her to be able to?

Things turned bad between Adriana and me about a year or two in. I only stayed as long as I did because I got comfortable and I was afraid to be all on my own.

She never understood me. I wore black nail polish once and she asked me if I was sure that my problem wasn't that I was attracted to guys. I was surprised by the question. I told her that wasn't it at all. In the beginning there was something inspiring to me about her—how well she took care of herself—her looks, her body, our lifestyle. She had so much energy and drive. After a while, I realized that neither of us was really connecting with each other—it was all surface level. We weren't just on different pages, Adriana and me, but in unrelated books, on separate shelves, in different libraries.

I still wasn't ready to leave. It was the circumstances that forced me. A part of me thought that despite my misery I could've gone on living the way I did forever.

The breakup was like having that dead weight shoved into my throat as I was thrown head first into Lake Ontario. I couldn't say a word against her when I was the one who cheated. I was the one who wanted her to live a lie. I was the one who asked for more than I could give. I was the one who never really loved her.

The price I pay for my selfishness is the fear that this is it—that it will never work out with anyone, and that my life will never get better. I find it impossible to believe in love right now—that I can love anyone and that anyone can love me.

I think I need to stay away from Marli for a long time now. I think the only thing I'm capable of is hurting her. She's staying away from me, so I think she knows it too.

Occasionally I call Adriana and leave her messages. *Eu sinto sua*, I say, I miss you.

She never returns my calls.

Nicki

We talk on the phone today. I say, *I'll get a calling card, I want to speak to you.*

Alon suggests Skype, but I say no. *My microphone is terrible.*

I tell him the truth, about Lukas, about what's been happening with us, about how hard it's been to live here, about the terrible hostel. I apologize for cancelling my ticket to Israel, for not coming to see him.

He answers me in English. He says, *I know*, but he pronounces it, *I now.*

I laugh. I've forgotten how bad his English is. *I miss you so much*, I say, and I'm crying.

Fine, then come back to me, he says.

What? I ask him. *What about your girlfriend?*

Eizo chavera, he asks. What girlfriend.

I laugh. It's a weird involuntary reaction. I don't know what to say.

Really? I ask him. *What happened to her?*

It doesn't feel right, he says. *I wanted it to be the right thing, but it isn't. I still love you.*

I love you too, I say. I'm crying again.

So come home, he says. *Come back to me.*

I think about it. A part of me desperately wants to, but I'm scared that all the confidence I've found lately will disappear. I'm scared of losing everything I've built.

No, I say. *You come here. Toronto is interesting. I want you to see this place. It's really different to Israel. If you hate it after a few months, we can leave. If you like it, we can stay for a while. Plus, the weed here is great.*

He laughs.

But no hard drugs okay? I mean, I'm sure the acid here is great, and I know the coke is, my boss loves it, but only on occasions like New Year's or something.

He laughs again. *Okay. But anyway, I haven't been doing it so much anymore. I haven't had so much money lately. Plus it's less fun without you nagging me about it.*

I smile. I can picture him like he's standing right in front of me. I feel like burying my head in his chest. I can smell his skin. I can smell his sage deodorant. I want to kiss him. *Okay. So will you come here?*

Tni li lakhshov shnia, beseder? he says. Let me think for a second, okay?

He's quiet for what feels like ten minutes.

Alon?

Yes.

What are you thinking?

He pauses. *Why do they call you Nicki there?*

What do you mean?

It sounds so American. It's weird.

It's easier for them to pronounce.

Do I have to change my name too?

I laugh really hard. *No. Of course not. It sounds like the word alone. They'll just say the 'o' really hard.* I stop laughing. *Maybe I should go back to my real name, what do you think?*

I've always liked your name. Your name is who you are, Nili, he says. *I've been looking online while I talk to you. It's expensive to come there.*

How expensive, I ask him.

He tells me, and we work it out, in dollars. It really is a lot.

We organize for me to send some of the money to him by e-transfer in a day or two.

He says he feels terrible, but I tell him not to. We lived off his job for so long when I lived with him before.

It's my turn to give, I tell him. *It's my turn to invest in us.*

I think I can come, he says finally. *Give me about a week. I have things to organize here first. The girlfriend. The dogs. The job.*

Are you sure about this, I ask. *That's big stuff.*

Are you sure, he asks me.

I think so, I say. *Are you?*

I only do things that I'm sure about, he says.

He tells me he loves me, and I find myself saying it back, over and over. It's a relief to realize how much I mean it. Still,

I'm afraid of hurting him again. But what I fear most is not feeling satisfied.

Alon sends me an email a few days later with his flight information. It's in two and a half weeks. He says he's taking care of everything, and I know he means it. I've always felt that I can trust him.

I don't know what will happen when we actually get back together. I don't know if he'll hate it or love it here. I don't know if we'll be able to talk about our issues any more than we could before. I don't know if our love will be enough this time, but I know that we have to try this.

Dez

My life since I was a teenager has been one giant joyride of depravity.

I've had epic drunken sprees (everything from Cachaça to Absinthe), chemical benders (name the drug, I've smoked it or snorted it, stopping short only of heroin), had threesomes and even one orgy (as I recall there were eight of us, me, two other guys and five girls, and we all kept trading partners until we passed out from exhaustion at around six in the morning), tried every kind of sex, from the most vanilla to S&M (I even tried autoerotic asphyxiation once, where the girl tried to strangle me, to cut off the oxygen to my brain to make the experience more intense, which it did), but still, none of it ever felt as good or as long-lasting as cheating.

Cheating made you feel invincible. It let you avoid the pain of ever being alone and allowed you to never have to make a decision. It gave you instant gratification with no consequences. You didn't like her, didn't have such a good time? She expected you to call her every day? Fine, you never had to see her again. She no longer existed as far as you were concerned, and you knew that you'd see her on the street in two weeks or two months and not remember her at all, or at best only vaguely. In cheating there were no losses, only more experiences. I kept coasting, the buzz of adrenaline rising like a fever with every possibility of being caught, the frenzy, the heat intoxicating me more each time.

It's just sex, I told myself, and I craved it as often as possible. My drive was high, a day or two without it, a week at most, and I felt the terrible pinch travelling from my groin through my bloodstream, compelling and controlling me. Could I help it that women liked me? That I was naturally charming, that it was easy for me? I had a gift that I wanted to take advantage of while I still could.

Deus colocou o homem na terra para procriar, my father used to say, God put men on this earth to procreate. We were supposed to spread the seed. *No fim das contas somos todos animais.* We were animals after all.

I never really thought about how it would make Adriana feel because a part of me felt that she had tricked me, that she and my mother had conspired to force me into a bondage that I'd never fully agreed to. I resented her so much. I resented both of them. I was so angry for so long.

It wasn't that sex was boring; it was just infrequent and unsatisfying. It was never a challenge or even a distraction. It was her wifely duty, like that scene in the movie *Nineteen Eighty-Four*, a movie they showed at CDRR a few weeks ago, where the wife lifts up her skirt in the least sexy way possible. Her blow jobs really felt like jobs, like something I should've paid her to get over with.

I never felt like she was comfortable with me, or accepted who I really was. More than anything, it was the expectations. I was just a kid, I wasn't ready to provide for anyone else. I hadn't figured out who I wanted to be yet.

I hadn't figured out how to turn my love of having a good time into a viable, even lucrative career.

I wasn't trying to punish Adriana, at least not at first. I was just trying to gain control of my life, to affirm that no matter what she said or expected, she didn't get to control me. And it was really fucking fun, which was why I kept doing it too, because I could, and the rush was great, and at first she didn't seem to know, and then she didn't seem to care, at least not as much as she should have.

The truth is, if she had been crazy jealous, if she had cried or screamed or begged me to stop, I might have tried to. I wasn't a monster. But a part of me knew that like me, she was never emotionally invested in us.

By the time we got separated I was living in a pattern, a giddy loop, and even thinking about her cramped my lifestyle. It really felt better to me than anything: the feeling of spotting any hot girl—I didn't care about her hair or skin or body type, or accent or voice or personality, all women were beautiful to me then—deciding on her, and getting her. Having her once, or twice or even three times. Never calling her again, or calling her and leaving dirty messages on her machine. Buying sex toys or lingerie for her. Texting her to say that I wanted to stick it in her ass. Having one or two of her friends. Having threesomes at least once a week. I was living my fantasies and I was intoxicated.

I didn't think I'd actually fall in love. I didn't think I'd want to choose to live a different life. I don't even know what it is about Marlize—I mean she is special, but so is every woman when you take actual time to get to know them.

I can't say it's any one thing about her. I mean, I really love how strong and independent Marlize is, and in a real way. I think another part of it is the comfort factor. I can just talk to her. I don't know why but I've always trusted her. There's just an unspoken understanding. For some reason, she just gets me and lets me be, and I think I get her.

What I usually do if I think I like someone is try to read them, observe them, try to figure out what they need and want from a guy, then temporarily become it. Then after a short time, once I've gotten what I wanted, I get incredibly bored, and I dump her.

I don't want to manipulate Marlize. I want to walk around my apartment in my underwear, with my hair dirty, eating beans from cans and drinking wine straight from the bottle. I want to watch old TV shows in the dark, sing her old Portuguese kids' songs I remember from when I was young. I want to be able to get fat, or at least gain a few pounds in the gut and have her like it. I want her to gain a little too—she's what my mom would call dainty, so full of tiny bones, like a little fish.

I want her to feel like she can relax, like she can gain a little, or a lot, and I'll still find her beautiful. I want to hold hands and kiss without an audience. I want a life full of inside jokes and our own language. I want to do everything I can to try to make it happen.

Marlize

My old friend Lanelle sends me an email today asking me how I am. I don't know what to tell her. I don't know how to begin to describe the loneliness and the confusion, what it's like to fall in love and constantly fear losing the person. I still don't really know how she feels about the abortion. The last time I saw her, I was a kid. I really feel like a different person now.

I don't hear much from my father, or his new girlfriend the therapist. He sends me emails now and then, and calls occasionally, but we both find it hard to keep up conversation.

Lanelle is doing a degree in Speech Therapy that seems so much more specific and adult than what I'm studying.

The only question I can answer is what I miss about South Africa. I miss so much, the food, the drinks, the languages, the people. I miss drinking Sparletta cream soda, which in South Africa is green instead of pink. I miss Liquifruit fruit juices, being able to buy fresh guavas and granadillas everywhere, calamari steaks, which don't taste the same here, and South African wine. I miss shopping on Long Street in Cape Town, and seeing movies in the Labia Theatre.

I miss speaking my own language—how precise and expressive Afrikaans is. I miss using certain expressions—*gatvol*, for when you're really sick of something, *gemors*, for when something is a disaster. I miss Afrikaans soap operas like *Egoli* and *7 de Laan*, and advertisements being before and after a TV show, not during. I miss Afrikaans rock music, outdoor festivals like Obzfest, outdoor flea markets like the one in Greenpoint. I miss authentic Indian and Malaysian restaurants, places where you can have a curry and a spicy peri peri samosa for nearly nothing compared to here. I miss the cheaper beer. And clubs that let you in without even carding you, even if you're underage.

I miss my friends, and being able to smoke indoors. I miss the Cape Town Ballet, watching performances, the adrenaline of inspiration that strokes my soles. I miss the beaches, from Bakoven to Hout Bay.

Ek's verlang na Suid Afrika, I write to Lanelle. I am longing to go home.

Nicki

I talk to Dez after work. My shift ends at nine, and I decide to stay. I don't have anywhere else to go.

I sit on one of our bar stools, put my feet up against the bar panelling, get served like a demanding customer.

I pick at a pile of deep-fried spring rolls and a plate of calamari. I don't have the stomach for it anymore.

It's karaoke night, and a girl in skin-tight black pants and a New York Dolls t-shirt is singing "Kool Thing" by Sonic Youth as her friends cheer. I know the song; a guy I liked when I was in the army loved them. The girl's delivery is deadpan, her expression unreadable.

I look at Dez. He's grown a beard. It occurs to me that I've never seen him look this scruffy before. He has dark circles under his eyes, and his skin is pale. He looks like he hasn't slept in a few days. He's wearing a wrinkled Queens of the Stone Age t-shirt, with a blue button-down shirt over it, and green cargo shorts.

1998 called, I say. *They want their pants back.*

He slaps my arm lightly. *These pants are great.*

I watch the singer and say, *I could never be cool like her. I'm no good at being detached.*

He looks me up and down, appraising me. *That's true. You're the opposite of her. You're warm. If you ask me, warm is better. Warm is genuine. It makes people feel comfortable. Also, people know where they stand with you because you don't play games.*

I nod.

Girls like her, on Queen Street, in Toronto, in general are— what's that thing they say here—a dime a dozen. You're much more memorable.

I smile. *I'm not very good at being like other people, even if I sometimes really want to be.*

You're good at being you though, he says.

I laugh and shrug.

Sometimes I feel unbearably sad about my breakup. There are nights when I do nothing but cry until I pass out, followed by days where I feel strangely okay. I can never predict how my moods will swing, how something will remind me of Lukas, and the crying will start, out of control.

Sometimes the emotions are too much, I tell Dez. *I don't know how to do anything except fake being okay until it becomes true. I don't know how to live with myself.*

You're mourning the loss of a relationship, babe. Believe me, I'm going through the same thing. It's normal to feel like that. Your feelings aren't going to kill you. You just have to sit with them until they pass. That's what I'm trying to learn how to do anyway. Toda passa eventualmente, *everything passes eventually, as my mom would say.*

You met Lukas, right? I ask him.

He nods, *Yeah, once or twice. I only really talked to him the one time.*

What did you think of him? Did he seem like the kind of guy who'd turn on me? Who'd turn on me, and hit me? Could everyone else see it coming? Sometimes I feel like such an idiot.

He looks at me, rests his hand on my shoulder gently. *Nicki,* he says, *it's not your fault. The guy had problems. You couldn't have known. The truth about Lukas, aside from the hitting of course, is that he wasn't the right guy for you. Maybe he was nice sometimes, I mean, he had to have been, right? But he was a boy. You're a woman, Nicki.*

I nod, try to take this in.

A lot of the men in Israel were macho, masculine and tough-talking. Maybe it was their years in the army. When I first met Lukas, he seemed softer, more sensitive than a lot of men I'd met. I didn't know what kind of man I wanted, but I knew I wanted to be with someone more honest, someone who could tell me what they were feeling, who could talk to me. Maybe Dez was right. Maybe Lukas wasn't mature enough to face his past. Maybe he hadn't just been lying to me, but he'd been in denial himself.

My ex-boyfriend Alon is arriving in three days, I tell Dez. *We've been talking about getting back together. I used to think he was my great love. And maybe he still could be. He's never been to Canada; I don't think he ever even wanted to, and now he's coming here, just for me. I have no idea what I'm going to do if it doesn't work out.*

You have to go through with it, he says. *It's brave to tell someone you loved that you still believe and that you still want to try. Do you still love him?*

I nod, smile a little.

So, how bad could it be? No matter what happens?

That's true, I say.

He looks like he wants to cry when I mention Marlize. I had just seen her the day before.

I miss her so much, he says.

I want to slap him. *Then call her already,* I say. Dy kvar, *enough already, enough with the space. Pick up the phone.*

I have to admit that a part of me is happy to see him struggle, after seeing him get any girl he wanted every night. The one girl he really wants won't talk to him. There's something satisfying about it, the feeling that some kind of divine justice is being served, which fills with me with guilt when I realize it. Dez is my boss and he's supposed to be my friend.

I love being in love, I tell him.

He nods. *I hate it,* he says and makes a face. *I hate all the worry about what someone else is feeling, this crippling insecurity, this tightness in my chest. Look what happens when it goes wrong. Divorce is a terrible thing, let me tell you. You really think it's worth it?*

I shake my head. *I have no idea. I want to believe that these kinds of risks are worth it.*

He nods, goes to serve someone else.

I'm afraid to be alone, I tell him when he gets back. *I'm afraid to spend hours in my own company, talking to myself. I'm afraid to spend the rest of my life falling into convenient situations that work out badly because I was too impulsive. You think I don't know what I'm doing? I do. I sometimes wonder if I'll ever be able to be with anyone if I stop to think about and acknowledge who they really are. I wonder if I'm actually compatible with anyone.*

Dez is silent for a moment, fear clouding his eyes. *That I understand*, he says, and looks away.

I get up to leave, and then remember that I have something for him. I've been to Kensington Market, in one of those stores that sell hundreds of pins. I've got him a green and blue striped one for $2.50 that says, *Divorce is Expensive. Freedom is Priceless.*

I press it into his palm, and he laughs, flashing a dimple and the whitest teeth.

He leans over towards me, beaming, and kisses me on the cheek, and for a second I feel like the only other person in the bar. He pats my shoulder and whispers, *You're really something special, you know that, baby?*

I giggle. I can't help it.

You're going to be okay, I tell him. *You really are. But you need to call Marlize. She's going crazy. In Hebrew, we have this expression,* rachok meha'ayin, rachok mehalev. *It means that what's far from the eye is far from the heart. It's the opposite of what they say here about distance. You need to call her or she'll move on and forget about you.*

He nods. *Yeah, okay,* he says. *Okay, I'll call her. You're going to be okay too. If it doesn't work out with Alon, at least you tried. At least you'll know for sure.*

My stomach drops as I hear the words. *I don't think I'll know what to do with myself if it doesn't work,* I say. *I don't know if I'm strong enough to deal with that.*

You'll always be okay, Nicki, he says, looking surprised. *You're a lot stronger than you realize.*

Lukas

Moncton, New Brunswick is depressing. I got sick of buses and trains before I left Toronto, so I bought a beaten up ninety-six Dodge Shadow before I left. It was cheap as fuck and I was happy it made it all the way here. The outskirts are nice enough, full of these farmhouses and barns surrounded by massive pines, and green plastic mailboxes with the red arm that stands up when you've got mail. You can smell the sea, and there's vast, open space, but it's totally different from where I grew up. In Moncton all you see are signs of decay—strip clubs that advertise Tuesday night auditions for amateur night, tons of Popeye's Chicken and Wendy's, billboards about how to treat addiction on elementary school playgrounds. There's a couple of okay record stores, and a place full of '80s' memorabilia that Emily, my girl from Aurora, would've loved before Toronto swallowed her, but that's about it.

I find a pub near the water that serves typical Maritime fare—beer-battered haddock and fries, Keith's on tap. I have to eat and drink first—build up my courage for the big reunion.

I can't believe my mom chose to live here. Her boyfriend, Phil, must have family or friends here or something. I know I have nowheres else to go.

My mom seems nervous when I call her. I haven't seen her in over three years. She seems even more worried when I tell her I quit my job and want to crash with them until I get things figured out.

The unemployment rates are so high here, she says. I can hear Phil chiming in, in the background, but I can't actually hear what he's sayin'.

Motherfucker. I wonder if we'll get along.

When I pull up to the house I have to check the address twice. It's huge, with a porch and these boxy little green shrubs and yellow daisies growin' out front. It looks double the size of our house growin' up. There's a welcome mat at the door, a red stained-glass heart hangin' in the window. I ring the bell and wait.

My mom opens the door, more excited than I expect. She looks better than she has in years—clean clothes, a little thinner, hair pulled back in a ponytail.

She pulls me into a hug, then starts cryin'. I hold her as she shakes, as she struggles to get words, and then sentences out.

I'm emotional too.

Phil stands behind her, his expression blank, his body language uncertain. I tell him how glad I am to be there, how long the drive from Ontario was.

My mom puts her arm around me, and invites me in.

We have a lot to talk about, Phil says, and gestures to their living room couch, where my mom and I sit down. He sits in an armchair next to us.

I talk for a long time. It turns out I have a lot to say after all.

After about an hour, Phil shakes my hand.

I think they might actually let me stay.

Nicki

I take a GO bus from Union Station to the airport to pick up Alon.

I stare out the window at the high-rise condos and sidewalks packed with pedestrians and wonder what he'll think of this city.

With traffic and about fifty stops, it takes an hour and forty-five minutes to get there.

I don't know what to do with myself to pass the time. I make small talk with the teenagers sitting in front of me. I try to sleep. I get up to go to the washroom and pace the aisles. I dig around in my bag and find a worn-out collection of short stories by Etgar Keret that I bought in the train station in Tel Aviv.

It feels like a million years ago now.

I open the book randomly, to a story called "One Last Story And That's It."

I try to read but I can't concentrate on the words.

If I stop to think how I feel about him, my insides start unravelling, each new worry hooking onto and tangling with previous anxieties.

I don't know if I want to stay in this city.

I don't know how he'll feel when he gets here.

How he'll feel about me.

I don't know how I'll feel when I see him.

I wait an extra half an hour for Alon when I arrive at the airport. He emerges, finally, sweaty and exhausted, carrying a duffel bag. His long hair is tied up in a bun and held back with a hairband. He smiles when he sees me, his eyes glowing with excitement. He hugs me and I feel the tension drain from my body.

I squeeze him back hard and I don't want to let go.

What took you so long, I ask, and I'm alarmed to realize that I'm speaking to him in English.

Customs, he answers in Hebrew and we both start laughing.

I think of the time he came back from India with two bricks of hashish in his bag, and he was just waved through. *We need to teach them about hippies here,* I say.

Do you know what? I read the other day that a sign of learning a language well is thinking in it, and dreaming in it. Do you dream in English now too?

I have to think about it. *You know, I sometimes do,* I say, and I feel strangely happy about this realization.

He grins. *Do you dream about me in English?*

I don't know, actually, I say, and smile. *I think I mainly dream about you in Hebrew.*

He smiles. *Good answer.*

We decide to take a cab back to where I live.

We sit together in the backseat, our knees touching. He tells me about his flight, and the week leading up to his arrival. I rest my head on his shoulder. There's something about hearing so much of my own language that makes me feel like my feet are touching the ground.

I can't believe this traffic, he says, shaking his head as we crawl bumper to bumper on the Gardiner. *I thought Israeli traffic jams were the worst.*

I try to imagine us driving down the Ayalon Highway together. I feel a jolt of homesickness so fierce I will myself to look out the window.

The night sky is aglow with twinkling lights from hundreds of buildings' windows, towers and signs.

I think of the way Alon made the world open up to me when we went to India together.

I look at him closely. For the first time, I see possibility. His eyes are the colour of dusty hiking trails dotted with green leaves. I see us camping together on weekends, hiking in Canadian forests and national parks. I see us having kids one day, even if he never changes his mind about marriage.

I think about the way he grew up in the north of Israel, near the Lebanon border, in the eighties and nineties. I think about the trauma of his time in the army. I think of the reasons people have kids outside of Israel and for the first time, I understand it.

I squeeze his hand. *It's not so bad outside of downtown, or even outside of the city*, I tell him. *There's more nature, and less people.*

What do you like about this country, he asks me. I think of the way the sky sprays powdery glitter in the winter. I think of CDRR, of Dez, and Marlize, and even Lukas. I look out the window, and see people of ethnicities I can't even name.

It's full of people like us, I say. *People from different places, all trying to create a different life.*

He is quiet for a second, studying me.

Okay, he says gently. *Let's try.*

Dez

I haven't been able to stop crying. When I wake up I feel like someone has glued my eyelids together, and when I can finally pry them open and I stare at myself in my bathroom mirror I am shocked by how puffy my face looks. I never would've thought that it would be this hard to admit the truth—not just to my mom, or my sisters, or Adriana, or even Marlize, but to myself. I never thought it would be this difficult, to sit with myself, to know and admit all the things that I've done, to face it, and to do nothing. Not drink, not fuck some random chick, not build up to some kind of conquest that takes up space in my head, that distracts me until I forget about what bothers me—but to really sit with it.

Marli sends me a text. All it says is: *You're stronger than you think you are. I believe in you.*

She sends me another one two hours later that says: *I love you.*

I think I'm ready to see her tonight. Finally ready, even if I don't really deserve her.

This morning, when I go for a walk, I pass Bloor Street United Church, and a sign outside says: *God fell in love with you at first sight.*

Maybe he'll fall in love with me again someday. Anything's possible. At least I believe in possibility now.

Or maybe not. At least I'll know I was open to it.

When I see her later, I'll be ready to tell her that I love her. I've never meant it when I've said it to any other woman in my life—but maybe that'll make it special, more meaningful.

She is the first woman I've ever let myself love, who's ever let me love her.

I want her to love me. I want to be myself, completely myself with her, and have it be okay.

I go over the words she taught me so long ago, *Ek's lief vir jou*, I love you, in Afrikaans.

Eck's leaf fir yo. I want to say the words right. I remember the time she told me how everyone says *I love you* all the time in English, how it's stopped meaning anything, but how it's not overused in her language. I want to sound sincere.

A long time ago, I taught her the words, *Te amo*, I love you, in Portuguese. I wonder if she'll remember.

I hope so. It's the kind of thing I hope she remembers every day for as long as we're together.

Marlize

We are lying in the bed in his new apartment together. The space is small, but it's just his. The bed is narrow, but I'm just lean enough to be able to spoon him without falling out of it. He tells me that he wants it to be ours one day, that when the time is right, he wants me to move in. A September breeze blows through his open window. We have all our clothes on. He has his arms around me. My nose is pressed into his back. Our legs are wrapped around each other's. His feet are cold. He is passing-out tired, his eyelids closing. We have talked for hours, about everything. At one point he put his hands on my stomach and said he'd had nightmares about what had happened to me.

Just promise me, you'll tell me if we're ever in a situation like that again? No matter what happens.

I nod. *Good*, he says. *I don't want you to feel alone like that.*

I tell him about the nightmares I had at the time, about all my fears. He squeezes my hand.

Those things are scary, he says. *But I think everything happens at the right time.* He pauses. *Wait, you really imagined us having a son wearing a Brazilian football jersey?*

I smile.

Eu te adoro, he says. I adore you. He takes my mom's ring off my necklace, and it fits halfway on his ring finger. *I like symbols of commitment*, he says, which shocks me. *They're romantic. I actually never wore a ring with Adriana.*

Maybe one day I'll have it made into one for you, I say. *And I'll wear whatever you give me. I just want it to come from you.*

He smiles the biggest smile I've seen all night. *You know, I'm really lucky to be with you, Marli.*

The joy I'm feeling is too intense to express. *Me as well*, is all I can manage. *Me as well.*

I don't know what'll happen next month, or even next week. I don't know if I'll have to go back to South Africa when my student visa expires, if he'll cheat on me, if I'll have to go home and face my fears alone. If he'll go back with me or if we'll get married and stay here. Anything is possible. What I know is that we both want to try.

I want to fill my life with pleasure, and intense joy. I want to try to be more open like him, and like Claudette. I want to be passionate and take risks. I want to stop being afraid of really feeling anything.

I want to love him with everything I have.

We'll make love in the morning, first thing, liefie, he says to me, before he drifts off. *Or have sex, whatever you want.*

I smile. *I like both,* I tell him. *I haven't got that much experience yet*—he opens his eyes and looks at me—*but you're the best I've ever had.* He smiles, and closes his eyes again.

You're the most real I've ever had, he tells me. *The scariest, and in a lot of ways, the most beautiful.*

I don't know what's going to happen, but I'm not afraid anymore.

Te amo *Leo,* I whisper before I fall asleep. He squeezes my knee.

I'm going to live in each moment as it comes.

Acknowledgements

Thanks so much to my publisher, Quattro Books, especially to Allan Briesmaster for your insights, support and great conversations. Thanks so much to Luciano Iacobelli for believing in this novel, for your honesty and for your vision, and to Kristen and Natasha for all of your hard work. I appreciate it so much.

Sandra Kasturi, my editor. Thank you so much for understanding this book, its characters, and its concept from the beginning. Thank you for the amazing support and for the incredible attention to detail that made it all so much better.

Chris Bucci, my agent, thank you for being so positive and enthusiastic about this book from day one. Thanks for all the detailed feedback and for the time and discussion of all aspects of this book. It means the world to me.

Micah Vernon, my husband, who read every version of every sentence five hundred times, with undreamed of encouragement and support. Thank you for the daily inspiration, my love. I couldn't do anything without you.

Nurit, my mom, and Martin, my dad, who read early versions, discussed synonyms and the look of Queen Street in the middle of the night with me, examined early contracts and always believed that I could.

Ari, and Yoel, my brothers, whose hilarious turns of phrase couldn't help but make their way into several characters' mouths.

Thank you so much to my friends whose stories and help were invaluable to the writing of this novel:

Nicole Aube, for an amazingly close first reading.

Michelle Snook, Leanne Flynn, Lisa de Nikolits, Richard Rosenbaum, Jowita Bydlowska, Russell Smith, Liz Worth, Lynn Crosbie, Rene Bohnen, Dawn Promislow, Chad Pelley, Janette Platana, Antanas Sileika, Heather O'Neill, Maddy Curry, Sarah Beaudin, Shirarose Wilensky, Douglas Glover, Dave McGimpsey, Anna David, Kayla Short, Heather Wood.

Cathleen With, Richard Scrimger and Zoe Whitall for the amazingly kind words and inspiration.

Aryan Kaganof, Michelle Mcgrane, Toast Coetzer and Melinda Ferguson.

Pri Antunes, Luiz Baio Filho, Thais Silva, Leonardo Picano Dias, Claudia Haddad Leon and Cesar Martins were essential in both the Portuguese translations, Brazilian slang and turns of phrase, and the descriptions of Belo Horizonte. I can't thank you enough.

Yael Bronner Rubin's detailed recollections of her trip to India (among a hundred other useful Israeli stories, early reading and much more help in life than I can ever say here. I love you).

Dereck Thibault's experiences working in a Halifax hospital.

Felix's amazing descriptions of Kentville.

Thanks most of all to you, for reading.

Other Recent Quattro Fiction